Pablo Piñero Stillman. ..... master at rendering the unreliable narrator. Like a sleight-of-hand artist working the land of the short story, his characters shift and shape right before your very eyes before you understand how he's done it. You'll so enjoy getting taken. Step up to the main attraction, take a spin, see this marvelous show. It's worth it. Trust me.

—Sherrie Flick, author of *Thank Your Lucky Stars* and *Whiskey, Etc.*

Like the best of Antunes or Cortazar or Keret, these stories are beautifully weird and alive like magical alleyways that twist and turn, threads that ravel and unravel. They feel all at once intimate and familiar and fun and big and surprising and vital.

—Matt Fogarty, author of *Maybe Mermaids & Robots Are Lonely*

In Stillmann's Mexico City, you'd probably have to keep changing your clocks. It's a place of complex contingency, of brief and lovely collision. These are new stories, and Stillmann has wonderfully new ways to tell them. But for me the best of the pleasures are probably old school: rich immersion and the thrill of a line of clean sense. He's such an instinctively purposeful writer. Nothing goes slack in these stories. No sentence. No phrase. I loved this book.

—Scott Garson, author of *Is That You, John Wayne?*

Like the title itself, the stories in Pablo Piñero Stillmann's *Our Brains and the Brains of Miniature Sharks* are strange, vivid, and utterly original, rendered in a language that is straightforward and lyrical at once. Whether dealing with behind-the-scenes dramas of morning TV shows, a child coping with divorce, or an untethered man in outer space, these stories are about human connection, however inevitable or impossible. Inventive, hilarious and unexpectedly moving, Stillmann's collection is a book you won't forget.

—Lysley Tenorio, author of *The Son of Good Fortune*

OUR BRAINS
AND THE BRAINS
OF MINIATURE SHARKS

PABLO PIÑERO STILLMANN

THE 2019 MOON CITY SHORT FICTION AWARD

MOON CITY PRESS
Department of English
Missouri State University
901 South National Avenue
Springfield, Missouri 65897

First Edition
Copyright © 2020 by Pablo Piñero Stillmann
All rights reserved.
Published by Moon City Press, Springfield, Missouri, USA, in 2020.

Library of Congress Cataloging-in-Publication Data

Stillmann, Pablo Piñero.
our brains and the brains of miniature sharks: stories/
stillmann, pablo piñero, 1982-

2020931900
Further Library of Congress information is available upon request.

ISBN-10: 0-913785-95-4
ISBN-13: 978-0-913785-95-9

Cover designed by Charli Barnes,
featuring *Sad Shark* by Renata Galindo, Digital, 2019.

Typesetting designed by Michael Czyzniejewski
Text edited by Karen Craigo

Author Photo by Renata Galindo, 2019

Manufactured in the United States of America.

www.mooncitypress.com

Para Andrés, Lucía & Valeria

Contents

OUR BRAINS
AND THE BRAINS
OF MINIATURE SHARKS

VERSUS THE BROWN SOCKS

I spent the first few months of my parents' divorce alone, mostly in front of the television. Whereas my father already lived with his new girlfriend, my mother was busy with work, visits to the psychiatrist (some of them emergencies), meetings with her lawyer, and coffee dates with friends to update them on the comings and goings of the legal process. Nieves, a robust and grumpy housekeeper, made me lunch every day and looked after me until my mother got home at night.

I spent those afternoons watching all sorts of kids' shows. One was a Bulgarian series about a magician named Zslorya who saved children from dangerous situations. The rescue always involved a magic trick, and at the end of the episode the magician would explain the trick to the viewers. I also watched lots of baseball because Frecuencia 8, for some reason, showed all the Cleveland Indians' home games. After all this time I still haven't been able to forget some names from that mediocre squad: Carlos Baerga, Keith Hernandez, Sandy Alomar, Greg Swindell.

But my favorite show, the one I never missed, was *Buenas tardes con Omar*. Remembering that show is like remembering a dream: hazy, confusing, and saturated with emotions. When it came on, five or six p.m., I'd move from the upstairs television downstairs to my mother's room. I shouted to Nieves that I was going to do my homework, but she didn't care; she was watching her own programming on the kitchen set, an old contraption with knobs that used to belong to my great-aunt. I watched Buenas tardes con Omar in my mother's room, with the door locked, because, at nine years old, I was embarrassed to watch a show that was, in my opinion, aimed at little kids.

Omar, a bald man in a sky-blue sweater vest over a white shirt and black tie, sat behind a table covered with toys. I don't really remember a lot of what he did. He sang, read viewer mail, maybe told riddles.

What kept me tuning in to that show religiously was "The Adventures of Débora and Gastón." Débora was a white sock puppet on Omar's right hand, and Gastón a red sock puppet on his left. Débora and Gastón were orphans. Or they were trying to find their parents. Something like that. The important thing was that these two socks traveled the world and had all sorts of adventures. The villains were represented by other hands that showed up from both sides of the screen wearing brown and tan socks, the type of socks only worn by adults who've given up on life. So every day, Débora and Gastón were stuck atop the Eiffel Tower, or had mistakenly boarded a boat headed for Senegal, or needed to deliver a package to the Japanese emperor.

I can still feel the excitement of watching those socks come to life. There was a tingle in my hands, a knot in my stomach. As soon as the segment began, I was no longer in my sad existence, but was transported onto an inflatable kayak on Lake Peipus or a hot air balloon over Mount Kangchenjunga. Débora and Gastón felt to me more human than my parents, my teachers, or my classmates.

Besides being a peerless broadcaster, Omar was a phenomenal writer. While shows of that era—e.g. Zslorya's—consisted of standalone episodes, "The Adventures …" was serialized. At the end of Monday's segment, one had no idea how the siblings would escape their troubles until the start of Tuesday's segment. Each adventure was a puzzle. During the twenty-four hours between Omar's shows, or seventy-two from Friday to Monday, I, along with tens of thousands of other children, racked my brain thinking of how my favorite socks would wiggle out of their latest imbroglio. If a brown sock had trapped them under the Sphinx of Giza, then I'd spend a lot of my school day—at a corner desk, so my classmates and teacher wouldn't catch on—writing the script of Gastón and Débora's escape from the Sphinx of Giza. My solutions never held a candle to Omar's.

"The Adventures …" really hit its stride toward February of '91. The structure of the episodes changed: Instead of lasting one tight six-minute segment, sometimes the socks would eat up two or three segments of *Buenas tardes con Omar*. I became even more obsessed with these stories, even though some of the time I had no idea what was happening. (I didn't understand this as a boy, but "The Adventures …" had adopted the abstract quality of real life.) How was it that Gastón and Débora were in the Gunnuhver hot springs if we'd last seen them eating pupusas in Cuscatlán? In one episode, our protagonists stole a time machine from an independent scientist's illegal laboratory. This allowed the socks to travel to Ancient Greece and also to witness the implantation of Christianity in the Roman Empire. They also attempted, without luck, to thwart Ivan the Terrible's massacre at Novgorod. By then, Omar had forgotten about scripts—maybe also about the audience and the cameras—and would now solely improvise.

Without a doubt, the best plotline of "The Adventures …" came during this jazz age of the show. A tan sock stole a Vermeer painting, *The Allegory of Faith*, from a New York museum, sold it, and, with the money, hired a group of mercenaries to time-travel with him to the Haitian revolution to quell the slave uprising. Gastón and Débora, of course, went after him.

Although Omar's story was peppered with fantasy—Vermeer, for example, who died in the 1600s, showed up in eighteenth-century Haiti armed with knives to kill a landowner and burn his papaya farm—to this day I know more about the Haitian revolution than about the one that took place in my own country.

In one of the Haitian plotline's many climaxes, Gastón and Débora were tied to the trunk of a palm tree while the mercenaries danced, sang, and doused them in gasoline. They couldn't yet burn them alive because Captain Beaulieu, who was on his way aboard a horse, had the matches.

Then there was a commercial break. Let's say the first ad was for cookies. The next one for powdered milk. After that, maybe, there was an ad for whole-wheat bread, which was all the rage back then. Then came an ad for kids' toothpaste. My love for television had turned me into a commercial break expert. I knew that during *Buenas tardes con Omar* the breaks were made up of between three and four ads lasting thirty seconds each. After the last ad came a fifteen-second ID. And just as expected, the toothpaste ad was followed by the station's logo accompanied by a deep voice that said, *Telecapital: Honored to be in your home.* But after that came another ad. I sat up. Then came a station ID in which Telecapital wished its viewers a merry Christmas. In March? And another, this one congratulating President Batoner on his successful fifth year in office. Then an ad for a doll that needed its diaper changed. Then one for instant coffee. Then, again, an ad for a doll that needed its diaper changed. Then another one for the instant coffee. *Telecapital: Honored to be in your home.* Then ….

The commercials lasted until the beginning of the next show. I had one of those anxiety attacks I'd seen my mother get: dry mouth, brain reeling, body unable to stay put. For a moment I thought of asking Nieves what she thought had happened with Omar, but I hated her and, more importantly, I was certain she hated me, too. (Nieves and I rarely spoke, and sometimes I would catch her glaring at me.) I wasn't actually worried about Omar, though. He was omnipotent. What terrified me was that I would never know how (or even if!) Gastón and Débora escaped from the Haitian palm tree.

My mother would get home at night, exhausted, and immediately run a bath. I remember that night as the only one in which I looked forward to her arrival. In complete hysterics, I'd already looked up Telecapital in the phone book and called to demand an explanation. The receptionist hung up on me. I hadn't changed the channel, certain that Omar would eventually show up to assure us, his disciples, that all was well in his kingdom. But Omar never did, so I hoped that my mother would be able to explain the never-ending commercial break. Maybe it was something very common in television and I had nothing to worry about.

I heard the front door open and my mother exchanging a few words with Nieves, who then left. I would've run to her, but I didn't want to lose sight of the screen. When my mother finally appeared, she looked haggard: disheveled hair and smeared makeup. She sat on the bed.

"Hug me," she said. Then she began to cry.

I did as she said, all the while not taking my eyes off the screen, feeling the warm tears accumulate on my right shoulder.

Once she stopped crying, my mother went into the bathroom to run her bath. I stayed on her bed waiting for Omar. The room filled with the smell of Marlboros. Every once in a while I heard my mother's sobs bouncing against the tile. I stayed that way, hooked to Telecapital, until I fell asleep under the exhaustion of so much anxiety.

The next day in school, not able to talk to my classmates about Omar's mysterious disappearance, I spent all classes writing scripts in my notebook. Each one was crazier than the next, probably as a tribute to my hero. The math teacher called me up to the board, but I refused to obey. He insisted. I called him a tyrant—an insult I'd heard Débora hurl at Charles Leclerc—and ended up at the vice principal's office.

Of course that afternoon, when it came time for *Buenas tardes con Omar*, I ran down to my mother's room, locked the door and turned on the television. I couldn't believe my eyes. Instead of my favorite show, there was a cartoon starring a mermaid.

I never found out what happened to Omar. Things were very different back then. If a media company as powerful as Telecapital didn't want people to know something—it could be as serious as the murder of a political activist or as banal as a reason for a show's cancellation—then the people didn't know and that was that. Sometimes I'll bring his name up at dinner parties, just as a fishing expedition, but those who were fans of Omar usually just repeat the same old rumors, most violent or sexual in nature, none confirmed.

For weeks, every day at five or six p.m., I turned on the television, just in case. I'd never hated anyone like I hated that stupid mermaid. I now thought of Gastón and Débora more than ever.

Then came the apocalyptic rains of 1991, the ones people still talk about with a quivering voice. I was just a kid, had no sense of the meaning of either danger or loss. In fact, I celebrated the second deluge, the one in which more than fifty people lost their lives, because it led to schools being shut down for a week.

I spent the first two days of that impromptu vacation lying on the sofa watching television. I didn't shower or brush my teeth and I peed on the potted tree next to the window from where I could continue watching Zslorya or the Cleveland Indians. I would've gladly stayed in my pajamas the whole week, but the judge in charge of my parents' case, seizing on the school shutdowns, summoned me to testify on Wednesday.

That morning my mother dressed me in a corduroy jacket and a clip-on tie. She parted my hair down the middle, which was, according to Omar, how Captain Beaulieu did his hair. In the car ride over, my mother coached me on how to respond to the judge's questions. *Tell him we eat lunch together every day. Tell him I check your homework after dinner. Tell him I'm tough but fair. Tell him you love Nieves like a second mother.* At stoplights, she'd apply her makeup.

My father was waiting for us at the bottom of the stairs that led to the courthouse. As always, he had on a suit and a bowtie and held his briefcase in his left hand.

I hadn't seen the man since he'd left and couldn't bear to look him in the eyes.

"You're not going to say hello to me?" he said. It made me feel as if it were my fault that he'd been taken away from important things—meetings, conferences, long-distance calls—to go to the courthouse.

My parents left me in a drab waiting room along with the other children. Apparently, all the judges had called in the sons and daughters of broken homes during those days of no school.

There were no more free chairs, so I sat on the floor. From there I noticed that the men who worked at the courthouse all wore brown or tan socks, the women brown or tan stockings.

It was beginning to make me angry that my mother hadn't thought of telling me to bring the sports section of the newspaper or something to keep me entertained, when I heard a high-pitched voice call my name. It was Danila, a girl from my class. Danila never spoke to me in school, she was pretty and popular, but that day she had no choice. There was, magically, an empty chair next to her where she invited me to sit.

"Are your parents getting a divorce?" she said. She was wearing a red velvet dress and white ballet shoes.

"Yours, too?"

"I already testified," said Danila. "It's not a big deal."

"Why are you still here?"

She pointed to a teenager in a black sweatshirt playing with a handheld console. "Just waiting for my brother."

Danila and I talked for a long time. She even laughed when I impersonated our English teacher, a hunchback with a conspicuous hearing aid. Danila and I played hangman using crayons and paper the courthouse placed on a table to accommodate the children. The crayons were all broken and the paper was thick. Every once in a while, a woman with dyed auburn hair walked in to call a child. *Lemmy Vila, Rogelio. Rojano Obregón, María.*

I was so happy with Danila that I never wanted to be called. Sure, she'd been forced to hang out with me, but maybe now she saw how funny and smart I was and would also be my friend at school. Maybe she could even be my girlfriend.

After a round of hangman, Danila squinted toward the corner opposite us and smiled.

"Look," she said, "Carlos is here, too."

Carlos Gama was in our grade but not in our class. All I knew of him was that he'd been a finalist in a regional geography contest. The principal had called him up during a school assembly to congratulate him. Carlos had a sheaf of papers on his lap and drew with great con- centration, switching crayons often.

I was disappointed when Danila suggested we go over to say hello, as I wanted her all to myself, playing hang- man until the end of time. Why had Carlos's parents also decided to get a divorce?

"Be quiet when we go over," said Danila. "I want to scare him."

We left our things on the chairs and walked slowly to Carlos. He didn't see us coming and once we were a meter or so away I noticed what he was drawing: two oblong figures, one white and one red, both with googly eyes, who were crying because they were tied to a palm tree. Captain Beaulieu stood to the side holding a flaming torch.

Carlos became startled when he finally saw us and rushed to cover the drawing with both hands. "What are you doing here?" he said.

"Our parents are all getting divorced," said Danila.

I asked Carlos what he was drawing.

"Nothing," he said crumpling the paper.

In the only telepathic experience I've had—probably the only one I will ever have—Danila's brain linked to mine. The information wasn't transmitted in words, but in images. I saw her hiding in her basement watching Omar on a small television. I'm sure I transmitted an image to her as well. The connection didn't last more than a second.

"We're over there playing hangman if you want to join us," said Danila.

Carlos's face turned beet red.

A few minutes later, the woman with the auburn hair yelled my name.

THE LONGEST EARTHQUAKE

1.

My grandfather drew maps back when maps were hand drawn. Were he alive today he'd be useless like you and me. Or maybe he'd be a satellite. That was a joke. I'm not very funny.

2.

I won't use names in the telling of this story—except for Valenzuela, as a way to honor it—for a couple of reasons. First of all, this already feels exploitative. The second reason is that it gives me an excuse to use a map key. It will not come as a shock to you that I was never a great student. I dreaded school, but I remember the day they taught us to make map keys as a rare good day in which my talents were actually put to use. This probably had to do with the fact that I knew I was the granddaughter of a great illustrator of maps. I've never made a map key since then, so I'll incorporate one into this story even though, let's be honest, it is an impractical decision. It is also arbitrary as I could, for example, refer to my grandfather as "my grandfather," without using his name, as I already did in the previous section and in this same sentence and will later do with my uncle and father.

3. KEY

Any symbolism other than that which is actually stated is purely coincidental and should not be taken into account.

✪ My grandfather	❱ My grandmother
❖ ✪'s home country	✜ The city where I was born
Φ President of ❖(19**-**)	▲ The country where I was born

4.

✪ left ❖ when Φ rose to power. He'd just graduated from a prestigious school of fine arts and urged all his family to leave with him. *You're so dramatic*, they told him. *Must be the artist's curse!* And they weren't lying. ✪, a master of dimensions in his art, always had trouble judging the size and importance of outside threats. (This played an important role in the churrería incident.) But this time he'd be proven right. Even a broken clock, as they say. Did he actually have information to back up the claim that Φ would turn ❖ into hell on Earth? No. ✪ actually knew very little about politics. He loved art and only art, had spent every moment of the previous four years either painting, in class, or with his nose in the expensive art books his mother bought for him even though they couldn't afford them. Strictly speaking his relatives made a mistake, sure, but ✪ had already cried wolf several times by then. A couple of years before he'd foreseen The End of Money in a column thus titled in his university newspaper. He also went around explaining to anyone who would listen that the proliferation of long waves from the increasing use of radios would have disastrous effects on the brain's electric charges.

5. A LONGISH SORT OF PROLOGUE ONCE THE STORY IS ALREADY UNDERWAY

It must be addressed that I am telling you a story about a man I never met. How is this possible? Did I conduct a series of extensive interviews and rifle through documents in government offices? This wasn't necessary. Though it might sound impossible, I've had a close relationship with ✪ from a very early age. He's always been present through his absence. Everyone in my family has views—some more nuanced than others—on if what he did was wrong. More specifically, my uncle has always loathed ✪, and so his wife and children loathe ✪ too; my father, on the other hand, has always maintained that it's impossible to judge a man who lived through so much. I used to think this way myself, but witnessing the consequences of his actions has angered me. "Hurt people hurt people," say the self-help gurus. I agree. Still, all my negative feelings regarding him are tinged with guilt. It's not easy to hate Job.

Another way in which I've had a close relationship with ✪ is that the few people I know who knew him all say

I remind them of him. I have, they say, his creative drive, his anxious mannerisms and his dry sense of humor. (I said before that I wasn't funny. This was a lie. Why did I lie to you? Maybe we were getting too close and it scared me.) And the last way that I've had a relationship with this ghost is that everyone in my family (with the exception of ◗) is constantly talking about him. *Did you know that ✪ once got into a fistfight with a policeman? Is it true that he once told ◗ that he believed in astrology? For whom do you think ✪ would vote in the upcoming elections? Can you imagine what ✪ would think of our cousin's new boyfriend?* (I'd say he serves as our map if it weren't an imperfect and 1000 percent corny metaphor.) So I've been able to connect the bits and pieces to tell this story as it probably happened. We all do this with our families; we fill in the blanks. Unfortunately, not much can be gleaned from the journals that one of my cousins found in a box in ◗'s basement. They're mostly sketches of people and places with a few terse statements here and there. If something is so mysterious that I have no clue why or how it happened, I won't just make something up. No more lying. This is my promise to you.

6.

One of these impenetrable mysteries is why ✪ chose to come to ✤ since pretty much anywhere else would've provided less of a culture shock. ✪'s hometown was a quiet and reserved little village. Here in ✤, people communicate by shouting and need loud music in the background in order to carry out almost any task. *Idiots are loud*, he would always say. He also had to get accustomed to the humid subtropical climate and the suffocating corruption.

7.

☺ rented an apartment above a pharmacy just outside of downtown. As he was extremely talented, he had no trouble finding work as an illustrator for newspapers and magazines. He quickly became known for his maps. During the first few years he lived in ⊕, all ☯ did was draw maps in the spare room he used as an office with classical music playing on his Sterling to drown out the street noise. He barely spent any money and never really spoke with anyone except for the Valenzuelas, the married couple who owned the pharmacy (with whom he communicated in broken English), and who sold him a tonic that he swore made him more creative. The reason ☯ did nothing but work was that he thought of this time in his life as a parenthetical. After all, one of two things was bound to happen soon:

A. Φ would show his true colors, finally scaring ☯'s family, who would all immediately join ☯ in ⊕.

B. Φ would turn out not to be so bad after all, and ☯ would be able return to ❖ and continue his life where he'd left off.

8.

✪ got free subscriptions to the three newspapers he drew for: *El Liberal*, *El Nacional*, and *Nuevo Siglo*. He learned Spanish by poring through the international news sections of these three periodicals for updates on what was happening in ❖. Whenever Φ would do or say something crazy, ✪ scribbled a letter to his family and ran to the post office to mail it. *Φ did this awful thing! I told you! Come join me immediately! It will only get worse!* It breaks my heart to think how much he missed and worried for his family, how completely alone he was in ⊕. His relatives wrote back dismissing the warnings. The foreign press had no clue about what was happening in ❖. They lied to sell papers. After reading these letters, ✪, head down, would go to the pharmacy to drink a glass of tonic while the Valenzuelas attempted to console him. But the only thing that really calmed ✪ down was drawing his maps. They had become his friends, his psychoanalyst, his vice. Every publisher, newspaper and magazine in ▲ wanted their maps to be drawn by him. The other illustrators didn't stand a chance. Like him, most were artists struggling to earn a living; unlike him, though, drawing maps for them was just a job, a means to an end, while for ✪ it meant nothing short of salvation. He found a solace in these illustrations that he'd never had with his paintings. His fee was the same as his competitors' and his product clearly superior. ✪'s only demand was that they not rush him. *If you need it done quickly hire someone else.* Upon starting a new map, his blood pressure lowered, his normally contracted face softened. ✪ spent as much time as he could on each one, not due to work ethic or pride, but out of fear that when he finished it he'd go mad.

9.

After his first term ended, Φ was reelected. Heartbroken, ✪ spent a fortune calling his family long distance. *Now* would they join him? He had enough money saved up and could help them set up a small business in ✠, a pastry shop or something. They wouldn't budge. *At least come visit*, they pleaded. *We miss you*. But ✪ was terrified of Φ. The mere thought of stepping into what was now Φ's country made him nervous.

10.

One evening ✪ went to the pharmacy for his daily tonic and was surprised to find that neither of the owners was behind the counter. Instead there was a young woman. Her half smile and almond-shaped eyes left him cold. *¿Qué necesita, señor?* He became a mute. All he could do was stare at her white blouse buttoned all the way to the top. ✪ could practically feel the silk against his fingers. And her hair! Charcoal black, parted and almost down to her waist. It was all too much. He'd been frequenting brothels since arriving in ✠, but he hadn't actually shared a bed with a lover, like humans do, since leaving ❖. He mumbled, then stuttered and finally escaped without his tonic.

11.

The realization came to him minutes later while he worked on a map of Burma. His head fell on one of the encyclopedias scattered on the desk. No, it couldn't be. Oh, God. Had that much time passed? He screamed into the encyclopedia. ☉ remembered the first time he spoke to Mr. Valenzuela. The man told him he had only one daughter, no sons. She was in the fourth grade. Wonderful student. This was that little girl. He did the math with his fingers. Now she was seventeen! Where had his youth gone? ☉ screamed once more. Were he the drinking type, he would've filled himself up with cheap whiskey. What he did instead was lock the door to his study and continue working on his maps. The harder he worked, the less he thought about the Valenzuela's girl, Φ, his family, his loneliness, and the passage of time. When he took a break to rest his eyes or eat a sandwich, all would come flooding back to him, so he stopped taking breaks. Upon finishing the maps he had to do for work, he continued drawing maps—maps of countries that didn't exist, of countries that should exist, of his apartment, of the brothels, of his genitals and brain, of heaven and hell and purgatory. He finally broke down in a crying fit. Who knows what else went on in that apartment during those days. It would be ridiculous not to think that he at least considered taking his own life.

12.

The Valenzuelas, who'd been seeing ✪ practically every day from Monday to Saturday for years, became worried when he stopped showing up to the pharmacy. Mrs. Valenzuela rang his doorbell and got no answer. A neighbor let her into the building. Now she knocked on the door. No luck there, either. She went to get a locksmith, and when he finally let her in, Mrs. Valenzuela found ✪ swaying in his rocking chair with dead eyes. *¿Qué le pasa? ¿Está enfermo?* (By then ✪ spoke with the Valenzuelas in Spanish.) Mrs. Valenzuela asked the locksmith to go get her daughter immediately and to tell her to bring some sedatives.

13.

Imagine ✪'s confusion when the first thing he saw as he woke up from his druggy sleep was the Valenzuela's daughter sitting at his bedside reading Thomas Mann. *Le preparé una sopa, señor.* She looked after him for a couple of days. There are many versions of what happened there. (As I said, ◗ doesn't like to talk about ✪.) The most romantic one says that while ✪ slept off his insanity, ◗ stepped into his study and was fascinated with what she saw. The most beautiful maps, of places real and imagined, hung on the wall, laid on the floor, overflowed the desk. This versión says that when ✪ opened his eyes, ◗ was already in love with him.

14. DISCLAIMER

What do I think of a man who's almost thirty falling in love with a seventeen-year-old? What do you think I think?

15.

By the time ✪'s relatives were finally convinced Φ was a madman, it was already too late—the son of a bitch put the whole country on lockdown. The letters that now came for ✪, instead of trying to calm him down, told terrible stories of the military tearing the country to pieces. This was when ✪'s chronic insomnia took hold, when he began spending whole nights in the living room crying, refusing to be consoled.

16.

The letters stopped coming. ✪ never heard from anyone back home ever again. (At least I don't think he did.) You and I know perfectly well what happened to them. When my uncle was born, ✪ suffered another psychic break. ◗ tended to him and the newborn baby simultaneously, as if she'd given birth to twins. The study became the baby's room, and the Valenzuelas let ✪, once he got better, use one of the back rooms of their pharmacy as an office. ✪ never fully stabilized. When he wasn't working he was either irritable, angry or asleep. No one has ever claimed that he was a good husband or father. ◗, in an effort to help him, found a group of refugees from ❖ that had escaped to ▲ just before the closing of the borders. These were people who, in a panic, left everything to jump on whatever boat was leaving and it turned out that their boats just happened to come here. They met Thursday nights at a cantina, and ✪ joined them a few times, but it only underscored his sense of isolation. He'd been living in ✚ for so long, made a life here, however small, that he (and the other refugees) felt he wasn't like them. After all, he'd never lived in ❖ under Φ and ❖ under Φ, was all they spoke of. The really sad thing is that it wasn't like ✪ felt like a local in ✚, either. He still thought people were too loud, the streets were too dirty, and he could never make himself care about the local soccer league.

17.

The hard question is: Was escaping Φ the right decision?

18.

By the time my father was born, ❖ was crumbling. Φ had inaugurated his official strongman dictatorship by invading his neighbor to the north, a war that continued, and now they were also being attacked from the east. The borders of ❖ were constantly changing and it became the biggest of international stories. ✪ had more work than ever. Not only was he the best map illustrator, but he was actually from ❖! There wasn't a single periodical that didn't want their maps of the conflict to be drawn by him. ✪, as always, worked tirelessly, but it no longer gave him respite from Reality—this was the ultimate tragedy: The two had merged. Here he finished his metamorphosis into becoming a full-on angry loner. He was constantly having angry outbursts and on weekend days ❱ and her boys had to leave the apartment because ⊙ spent Saturdays and Sundays resting in bed or lying on the living room couch.

19.

Soon after, the Valenzuelas closed down the pharmacy to retire in their native village. The space was rented to a man who turned it into what would become the most famous churrería in ✤. ⊙ had to rent a studio and buy a used Renault to drive to and from work. He barely knew how to drive, hated dealing with traffic, and frequently complained that this new, drab working space tamped down his creativity. And yet somehow it gets worse. The day the churrería opened—after weeks of noisy construction—the apartment began to shake. ⊙ came home for lunch and noticed a stack of plates in the kitchen was vibrating. There was a strange humming sound. He asked his wife if this was an earthquake. *It's the churrería.* All morning she'd been scared of how her husband would react to the shaking. *Did you tell them?* She had, in fact, gone down there, baby in her arms, to ask what was going on. They'd explained that they had some powerful machinery in the kitchen and that it was normal for the apartment above them to shake a bit. *Normal? They told you it was normal?*

20.

✪ was foaming at the mouth when he got to the churrería. He began by shouting and cursing at the employees. Or maybe at first he tried to tell them calmly, as
calmly as he could, that their machines were making his
apartment shake. They offered him free churros for his
troubles. Things got out of hand. *Have you no sense of
decency?* he must've said in his viscous accent. *You have
invaded my home!* Punches were thrown. ✪ spent a night
in jail. When they let him out, he went straight to his
landlord's office. *I'm sorry for the inconvenience*, said
the landlord. In his journals, ✪ writes that although the
people of ✢ always pretend to be polite, they are actually filled with aggression. *It's not a mere inconvenience*,
✪ said. Six months remained on his lease and he wanted
his money back so he could move his family into a
non-vibrating apartment. *Like I said, señor, I apologize
for the inconvenience and wish there were something I
could do. For the moment, however ....*

21.

He went straight to a payphone to call Mr. Valenzuela.
Maybe he was weeping. *How could you do this to me?*
(He must've, for the first time, now that things had forever changed, looked back fondly on his first years in
✢.) The Valenzuelas were rural folk. They hated ✢. Their
plan had always been to make just enough money with
the pharmacy to retire. ✪ knew about this plan, as his
friends had spoken about it to him many times over the

years, yet Mr. Valenzuela, calm as ever, explained the situation as if he were doing it for the very first time. The last thing ✪ ever said to his father-in-law was that he'd betrayed him.

22.

The family had no choice but to remain in the shaking apartment until the lease ran out. *It'll be the longest earthquake*, joked ☽, *and then things will go back to normal.* ✪ didn't laugh. (How long had it been since he'd laughed?) By then he had no idea what normal felt or looked like. Their children got used to the perennial vibration, and although it bothered ☽, she kept it quiet. For ✪, however, things were more complicated. It wasn't so much the shaking as the injustice of it all. Each time he felt the machines under him, it was a reminder that the world was rotten and unfair. His brain flared and his stomach tightened. He'd always kept to himself, did what he had to do, and never intruded on anyone else's life, yet others kept poking at his peace of mind. *All I ever wanted was to be left alone.* That's a phrase from one of his journals. I don't believe it. All he ever wanted was to love and be loved, but to admit this would've been too painful.

23.

I've racked my brain over the years trying to figure out why ✪ disappeared the same day he was finally liberated from the shaking apartment. Come up with your own theory as to where he went in his Renault and it'll be just as valid as the ones I continually trade with family members. He moved in with a mistress and started a family with her. He went back to ❖ to join the resistance that would eventually, after much fighting, topple Φ. He rented a motel room and shot himself. What I do know is that he was broken. I am broken, too. Believe me. My family was born from trauma. It's what we call home.

24. EPILOGUE (ANOTHER DISCLAIMER)

Unfortunately, I can't end this with that last sentence from the previous section. I'd feel guilty if I didn't stress that there are much more positive versions of ✪ out there. Ask my cousins to tell you about him and you'd think they were talking about a different person. Not long ago I was at a Halloween party and met the grandson of the man who used to be *Nuevo Siglo*'s managing editor back in ✪'s time. He was dressed as a baseball player and I was a pumpkin. He said that his grandfather, who lived to the age of ninety, used to tell him about ✪. They sometimes spoke at the newspaper's offices when ✪ went to deliver his maps. *He said that your grandfather was a brilliant and wise man*, said the baseball player. This type of thing has happened to me before. I just nod and tell them that ✪ was an exceptional man.

OUR BRAINS AND THE BRAINS
OF MINIATURE SHARKS

The number thirty-nine began appearing all over our beloved city.

I say beloved with a sad irony, for our city was shit.

Around that time I used a popular dating app with mixed results, but at least I was finally getting dates. Having always been a shy loner, there I was going out with this woman and that other woman to hip places where people drank mezcal and artisanal beer.

I can't really say with certainty where I saw my first thirty-nine. Gun to my head I'd say it was riding an Uber on my way to visit my mom. Stuck in the usual afternoon traffic, I looked out the window at a bus and noticed the number thirty-nine spray-painted on one of its windows. However, as Dr. Bengoechea loved to remind me, it's stupid to trust our brains. My mom was dying. Every time I went to the hospital I'd find her with bloodied tubes sticking out of her body. On my way to the hospital, surely, my brain was releasing all sorts of chemicals and ring all sorts of neurotransmitters, which might explain why that moment got cemented with such authority.

☾

The app was simple: If you weren't interested in a profile, you gave it an X; if you liked a profile, then you gave it a gold star. Should a person you gave a gold star give you a gold star as well, a window would open up so the two of you could chat and, eventually, if all went well, meet up.

Now that I think about it, it might be that the first thirty-nine I saw was at a bourgeois coffee shop called Doble Ele. Like any bourgeois coffee shop worth its salt, Doble Ele employed artsy folk who needed a flexible job to pay their share of the rent. One time when I went to pay for my coffee, the woman at the register—charcoal-dyed hair, green eyes, septum ring, and ennui—was drawing stylish thirty-nines all over her spiral notebook.

Dr. Bengoechea told me that, for some convoluted evolutionary reason, our brains are wired to remember interactions with people with green eyes more clearly than with those who don't have green eyes.

The main problem was I didn't like the women I went out with. They were nice—and obviously, because of how the app worked, I found them attractive. Some were smart, others funny, but there was always something missing. Being so bad at getting dates, I'd come to idealize them. A first date was more like a lottery ticket than a job interview.

☾

I was introduced to Dr. Bengoechea through a public radio piece on how once again psychiatrists worldwide were beginning to experiment with psilocybin mushrooms as a way to treat depression. They interviewed a group of researchers at the National Autonomous University of Mexico, who were conducting small-scale experiments with the psychedelic drug. It turned out that these researchers had hired Dr. Bengoechea as a consultant for the trials. During the piece he stood out as the most eloquent voice. Having battled depression all my life and being a sucker for a magic bullet, I immediately contacted him.

Was I asking too much of these women?

A truck carrying thirty-nine pigs overturned on the highway to Querétaro. The pigs that didn't die had to be shot. A man in a manic state tried, unsuccessfully, to highjack flight 039 just as it was about to take off from the Mexico City airport.

His office was a normal professor's office except that it was nested in a skyscraper at the heart of the business district. To get to him I had to leave my car with a valet, show an of official ID at the lobby, and wear my visitor's badge at all times. I walked in to find him looking out the window, eating pasta out of a glass container. One of the walls was a bookshelf packed with books, and the other was pure glass, separating the doctor's office from the lab where a couple of research assistants were going over some data on the whiteboard.

My rule was that I wouldn't even mention the whole thirty-nine affair until we ran out of topics. I didn't want to seem like some conspiracy-obsessed weirdo. Most of my dates kind of knew about the thirty-nines but had no interest in them. A deal breaker, however, was when a woman completely ignored them. *What do you mean thirty-nines appearing all over the city? I don't think I understand what you're trying to tell me.* One asked me if I was schizophrenic.

He wiped his mouth with the sleeve of his lab coat and asked me to sit down. I explained to him that although I was doing somewhat well at the moment, my life had been a constant uphill battle, with the hill being major depressive disorder. "I heard you talk on the radio about the psilocybin treatment." He plucked out a tablet from under the mounds of papers on his desk and used a stylus to make some notes while he questioned me. "What is your family history with depression?" "What is your employment history?" "Sex?" "How often do you feel anxious?" "When was your last depressive episode?" "Go over all the meals you eat on a normal day." "Intrusive thoughts?" "Any suicide attempts?" And so on. This took almost two hours. When we were done, Dr. Bengoechea said we'd have to continue meeting regularly so he could assess my case. "But we can't meet here. My bosses wouldn't like it."

The next time I saw him was at a cantina. Dr. Bengoechea loved soccer and wanted us to watch a Champions League game. That afternoon we talked about everything from international politics to our favorite books and, of course, we talked plenty of soccer. I didn't find this too odd because I'd seen psychiatrists before and this is usually what they did with me—albeit not in a cantina: talk about random things while they gauged my mental state. (It's a lot easier than gauging someone's mental state by just discussing their mental state.) The next time we met we went for breakfast. That was when Dr. Bengoechea told me about his family troubles and the whole thing with the miniature sharks.

Maybe I wasn't going out with the women I actually wanted to go out with. Because here's the thing, some women who used the app played hard to get. In those cases, afraid of appearing creepy or desperate, I backed off. These were extraordinarily beautiful women who seemed to have good jobs and a stable of friends. They didn't need the dating app. It just amused them. As for the women I went out with, the real world was a difficult place to navigate, and relationships, of any kind, were not easy to come by, so the app was The Way to Meet People. When dealing with women like that (like me), it was very simple to take that step from the chat to a date at a mezcalería.

☾

Thirty-nine billboards on the Periférico were covered up with black tarpaulins with a thirty-nine painted on each of them.

What followed is what one would expect: prep school, Swarthmore, medical degree from the University of Michigan, and residency in New York. He then got a position at Georgetown's Center for Brain Plasticity and Recovery, which catapulted him to his own lab at Walfrid University. Dr. Bengoechea was doing some truly revolutionary work dealing with the neuroplasticity of a rare species of miniature shark, rewiring their brains to make them not act like what they were, but more like swordfish, salmon, and, with a group of a dozen sharks, even succeeding in implanting the communal family structure of whales.

Those who've never tried online dating have severe misconceptions about it. *Isn't it superficial to filter potential partners based solely on physical appearance?* Humans have been doing that forever. (Besides, we all know that looks are much more than just looks.) What if you get a crazy person? It's surprisingly easy to spot a crazy person with just a few texting back-and-forths. Although I once did go out with a woman who was a bit off.

The buttons in many of the city's buildings' elevators were changed to all display the number thirty-nine.

☾

She was harmless, though. Still living with her very Catholic parents. Had an interest in the Talmud and performance art. Shortly after we said our good-byes, she texted me saying she'd made it home. Then she texted me again. And again. Then came some voice messages that didn't make any sense. One, for example, was her saying, in English, *Hey, Mr. Tambourine Man.* She dialed me at four in the morning. I didn't answer. Then she texted asking if I was still awake. I never heard from her again. Like I said, harmless.

An animal-rights group released pictures of the miniature sharks trapped in their tiny, filthy tanks, some wounded (a missing eye, a wounded fin), others fighting, most malnourished. Dr. Bengoechea swore that the photographs were staged and digitally altered, but Walfrid took away his laboratory and the doctor was ostracized from American academia, which is how he ended up in Mexico City doing research for a pharmaceutical company.

A congressional candidate was shot thirty-nine times. Our most renowned painter was interviewed by a newspaper and the answer he gave to every question was to just say "thirty-nine" in various languages. The next day, the painter disappeared.

"Depression," Dr. Bengoechea said as we walked the halls of the Museo Universitario de Arte Contemporáneo, "manifests itself in miniature sharks with an uncanny similarity to how it does in humans. Which is of course ironic because people are always using sharks as a lesson to always move forward without regard to environment or feelings. Though these are miniature sharks, so it's not that ironic."

Of course our meetings sometimes touched on the thirty-nines. Dr. Bengoechea was sure they were related to some sort of ultra left-wing organization. I accused him of being paranoid one time while at a Hungarian pastry place. "It's understandable. Traumatized by guerrillas, those groups now haunt you." Days before, I'd seen a man dressed in bright, expensive clothing walking outside a multiplex with a gold thirty-nine hanging from his neck. He looked more narco than anarcho. "So you think it's got to do with the drug war?" "Everything nowadays is in some way or other related to the drug war."

Then there was Lorenza. We were supposed to meet for lunch, but that morning she changed it to afternoon coffee. Then she canceled the coffee and turned it into drinks at eight. At seven fifty-five, as I handed my wet umbrella to the hostess, Lorenza texted me again saying she'd be a little late. When she got there at eight-thirty, I fell for her. Immediately. Physically, I mean. She was better looking than her profile. The first few minutes of our date was me rambling on about nothing while Lorenza seemed to wonder what was wrong with me.

☽

"Why didn't you ever marry, doctor?"
"You're not married either."
"But I'm only twenty-eight."
"I was twenty-eight once."

After the first hour or so things stabilized. We both liked Woody Allen and tried to talk about his movies even though once one has seen enough of them they all kind of meld into one infinite movie. *What's the one with Sean Penn? Oh! The musical one?* Everyone Says I Love You? *No, no, that's the one where they get hypnotized. You know the one I absolutely love? The one where he's a dictator. And time-travels, maybe?*

There was no way I was going to bring up the thirty-nines. Here I was, hitting it off with a beautiful woman. I didn't want to risk it. It was, however, becoming clear that she was what they call a high-functioning alcoholic. All her stories either dealt with her working until late in the night or drinking until early in the morning. She seemed to have an endless number of hangover remedies. Her drinks disappeared with tremendous speed.

We were at a burger place watching a Copa América game when I told the doctor I was getting impatient. I'd come from visiting my mother at the hospital. She wasn't doing well. Her husband's eyes told me she might go any day now, and it terrified me. Wasn't this the perfect time for the treatment? "Funny you bring it up," said Dr. Bengoechea. "I met with the researchers just yesterday morning and fought for you. It seems I've finally convinced them. Now all we need is to get the paperwork ready." I could feel my face glow with happiness.

She constantly flashed her big smile and listened to my stories with great attention. When I leaned over to kiss her my mind went empty. It felt liberating to defeat my thoughts with a pure act. Had I been completely honest, after that kiss I would've told Lorenza that I liked her in a way I didn't usually like women.

It still took me a few more meetings with Dr. Bengoechea to realize that he'd been lying to me. (Hope is a dangerous thing.) We went to a buffet at a five-star hotel, a reimagining of *Death of a Salesman* in which Willy Loman was a rabbit-human hybrid, a bike ride in the woods, a poetry reading. I woke up in the middle of the night having suddenly figured it out. I decided to do what I should've done long before: visit the actual UNAM researchers, the ones who maybe weren't as eloquent or intelligent as Dr. Bengochea, but who were more practical.

We ended up at my apartment. Unsurprisingly, sex with her was great.

Dr. Rosa Tobar kept me waiting outside her office for almost an hour while she met with a student and took a couple of phone calls. When I was finally let in, she asked me to make it quick, as she had a department meeting. Dr. Tobar's annoyance increased the more I talked. "How long has it been since your last depressive episode?" she finally interrupted me.

"Two years, maybe? I believe it was around November of—."

"I'm sorry to tell you, but—." I blurted out that my mother was about to die, and that maybe for that reason I was useful to the experiment. Dr. Tobar looked at her wall clock, then back at me.

"The psilocybin experiments were done with patients whose last major episode was no longer than six months prior."

"You said we're done?"

"There was a mishap with one of the patients and the study was postponed. Indefinitely."

"But Dr. Bengoechea …."

"Dr. Bengoechea," said Dr. Tobar, "was let go as a consultant shortly after that radio story aired. Animal rights groups called to inform us of his past actions, and a serious institution like this can't, well, you know."

The Angel of Independence is the city's central landmark, a twenty-foot golden statue that stands on a hundred-and-twenty-foot column. The angel holds a laurel crown up in front of her, as if offering it to the denizens of this chaotic place. El Ángel, of course, is supposed to represent all the idiotic and vague values those sorts of things always represent: courage, sovereignty, etc. One morning hundreds of people crowded below it as they noticed that the laurel crown had been substituted by a black thirty-nine.

"I need to come see you."
"Would you like to meet somewhere for lunch?"
"I'll meet you at your home when you're done with work."
"But—."
"What's the address?"
"There's a charming new taco place I've been wanting to go to."
"Doctor. Please."

I awoke at dawn to pee and found her getting dressed in the bathroom. It was then that I realized what had actually happened. I never saw Lorenza again.

Maybe it was because of his family history with wealth and power that I'd always pictured Dr. Bengoechea living in a nice, suburban brick house. But he lived in an old apartment building in one of those neighborhoods it's better not to walk at night. He opened the door wearing sweatpants, a robe, and slippers. I could tell he knew that I knew. My anger waned as soon as I saw the narrow apartment crowded with books of all colors and sizes. The only thing hanging from the walls was a single black-and-white framed picture of his family back in Peru.

☾

"Which one are you?"

He pointed to a tiny boy with a giant head wearing short pants, a plaid shirt, and a tie. "Sit down," he said. "I'll get you a beer."

What did I want from him? An apology? Was my goal to make him feel bad? All Dr. Bengoechea did—all he had done, ever, you could see it in his face— was feel bad. As did I. Why wasn't I in the hospital with my mother during her last days? We'd had our troubles, yes, but we loved each other. She'd die and I'd have to survive that death on my own, without the help of a miracle something or other. As for the thirty-nines, more would appear, then all would fade away.

THE FIRST MAN IN SPACE

Like all of his other accomplishments, the first man in space, floating above our planet, rationalized this feat into irrelevance: It had all happened because he'd blurted out the word "rope." Sadly, history, too, has undervalued Ian Donatien Fouroux's inaugural trip into space for reasons that are all too familiar for those living below the equator.

Fouroux's only two friends were Camila and Tito Mazzilli, a married couple, both of them renowned physicists, whom Fouroux met during his brief stint as a hashish dealer. The Mazzillis would often have him over for supper at their house, in the outskirts of Buenos Aires, where the three would eat steak and potatoes, drink generous amounts of wine, and get high. Fouroux, who was normally bored by social activities, spent countless hours at the Mazzillis' going up and down his list of cosmological queries. *What do you mean time and space feed off of each other? Has the universe always existed? Can you explain the twin paradox to me again?* (The exact nature of Fouroux's relationship with the Mazzillis remains murky. A recent biography of Camila cites anonymous sources to posit that the three were involved in some sort of intricate BDSM fantasy game, while an article written by a grandchild of the physicists argues that they only befriended the lovable loser out of pity.)

After a particularly heavy night of eating and drinking, the Mazzillis took their friend out to the shed to show him a project they'd been working on secretly. It was a transparent sphere with a sole leather chair inside. In front of the chair was a yoke, and atop the yoke they'd installed (what was then) an ultra-modern screen. Peppered throughout the outer dermis of the sphere were small yet powerful motors.

"That is either the ugliest or most beautiful thing I've ever seen," said Fouroux. "It brings to mind the cruelty of both life and death."

Tito lit a joint dipped in hydrocodone. He was so moved in so many ways by his and Camila's "child," as they referred to the sphere, that he could never be in its presence without some kind of anxiolytic. "It began as a joke," he explained. "But my wife and I are too serious for jokes."

"It can go up into and travel through space," said Camila. "We've done the math. It works."

Fouroux, who never doubted a word said by the Mazzillis, went up to the sphere and touched it with his open hand. He fogged the glass with his breath and drew a happy face with his finger. "And the fuel?"

"Excellent question," said Camila. She walked over to a dark corner and picked up another, smaller sphere. "It goes in this."

"It's not big enough," said Tito. "I mean, it's as big as it can be, but not big enough to carry the amount of fuel necessary for a round trip.

"We can send it there," said Camila, "but we can't bring it back."

Then, like possessed by the spirit of someone with self-confidence, Fouroux took a sip of wine and said, "Rope."

A thick silence floated into the shed. Then Tito: "A couple of hundred thousand kilometers of rope?"

"Why not?" asked his wife. The daughter of one of Latin America's richest men, she was used to asking that question. "You put the sphere out there and then you pull it back with the rope."

Tito and Camila would've had no problem carrying this out in the open, with permission from the government—they both considered themselves apolitical—but the military state would make them wait at least a year while they prepared the launching ceremony and neither of them had the patience. They were fortunate enough to have a good friend (one of Camila's ex-lovers) in the soon-to-be-defunct Ministry of Supraterrestrial Exploration, Martín Ronconi, who sneaked out the machinery necessary to launch the sphere to a soccer pitch near the Mazzillis' house.

Tito and Camila, who had been fighting about who would get to go up to space since the sphere had begun to become a reality, knew they'd made the right decision as they watched a smiling Fouroux, in his fire-retardant suit, screwing on his helmet.

"You know," said Camila to the impromptu pilot, "in another universe you are a cosmologist."

"And in another universe," said Tito, "you are a preacher."

"In another universe," said Camila, "you drive a taxi. You are a playwright, a dentist, a military dictator."

"In another universe," said Fouroux, his words echoing inside his helmet, "I am about to become the first man in space."

The sphere launched at around two in the morning, and we know very little about what happened next. We do know, though, that the farther away Fouroux got from the soccer field, from the outskirts of Buenos Aires, from Argentina, from Earth, the more he realized how inconsequential and incredibly crucial everything was. We know that he must have felt his soul expand until it pushed his heart, and that at some point it became crystal clear to him that all this time he'd been in love with Camila. We know he belittled himself. We know the rope broke, or disintegrated, or was cut by someone with a steak knife, and that Fouroux accepted his fate as he drifted away into nothingness, his memories expanding more and more until they finally disappeared.

POSTMODERN ACT
IN THE HISTORY OF RELIGION #22:
JAMES NAYLER RIDES
A DONKEY INTO BRISTOL

When I say he looked like Christ, and he most certainly did look like Christ, I mean he looked like our notion of what Christ looked like, which, as we all know, is not at all what Christ looked like. Impossible to know whether it was product of a manic episode or illumination from within, but Nayler rode a donkey into Bristol as his followers cried, "Holy, holy, holy." The People, of course, were outraged. What does one (I) mean when one (I) says (say) The People? The People: that ball of opaque gas that rests on our planet and yet is bigger than our planet, covers our planet, tries to convince us it is the planet. (One of life's defining questions is, "Am I part of The People?" Other defining questions are, "Do I want to be part of The People?" "Do I wish for my loved ones to attach themselves to The People?") The Parliament, voice of The People, ordered for Nayler to be stoned to death as is called for in Leviticus: And he that blasphemeth the name of the LORD, he shall surely be put to death, and all the congregation shall certainly stone him. The Practical Man, let's call him Thomas Cromwell, however, remarked that stoning Nayler to death would make him look a whole lot like Christ, with whom, as we know, he already bore a striking similarity. "It would be counterproductive," said Cromwell. "It would be falling into his trap," said Cromwell. "We might as well just crucify the man," said Cromwell, The Practical Man. (Also, privately, inside his practical head, Thomas Cromwell was asking himself defining questions: "Do I want to be the Romans?" "Is the leader of The People still considered part of The People?") "OK," said Parliament in one voice. "We won't stone him." To which The Practical Man, Cromwell, responded, "Phew." "We'll just give him a good flogging in the streets," said Parliament's collective voice. "Well," said Cromwell, The Practical Man, "don't you think that's still a little close to the plight of You-Know-Who?" "In addition to the flogging," said Parliament, una voce, "we demand his forehead be branded with the letter 'B'" "For blasphemy!" said a lone voice. Parliament cheered. "And I'd like to propose," said another lone, lost voice, "we pierce his tongue with a hot iron!" "Aye!" growled the Parliament. "Is that all?" said Cromwell, cynical, resigned, a bit dizzy. "No," said Parliament. "We have one last order: Nayler must be pilloried." "Pilloried?" "Pilloried!" "Pilloried?" It doesn't take a brilliant man to realize how much a pillory resembles a cross. Cromwell, The Practical Man, was more than brilliant. Cut to Thursday, Nayler attempts to chew a piece of rotten bread in his cell: long hair, beard, "B" engraved on his forehead, mutilated tongue. Yet he had a smile on his face. (Again, look somewhere else if you want to know the difference between madness and

The Light.) Our last chapter finds Nayler being released from prison and getting on a horse. "What will you do now?" said the very few of followers he still had. "Will you again challenge The Powers that Be?" "Sorry," said Nayler. "All I desire is to ride to Yorkshire and see my family." Completely understandable. But he never made it to Yorkshire. A group of highwaymen (knights of the road, thieves, criminals, Bad Guys) attacked him in the forest and left him for dead. A hermit came across Nayler minutes before his death, and the man who rode a donkey into Bristol uttered one of the most beautiful passages in the history of religion (edited here in the interest of brevity): There is a spirit which I feel that delights … but delights to … hope to enjoy its own … wrath … cruelty or whatever …. It sees the end … it conceives…it is betrayed …. Its crown is … life is everlasting love … its kingdom … and not … by lowliness of mind.

DARK, COLD, AND SUPPOSEDLY INFINITE

DORA

Agustín's only delivery that day was a set of angel's trumpets to Polanco, a neighborhood full of yoga enthusiasts and part-time vegans who fetishized capital-N Nature and thus wanted exotic plants to decorate their cool apartments.

It was a four-floor building, Spanish colonial, one place per floor with an elevator that called up directly into each apartment. A beautiful woman was waiting for him. No. Not beautiful. Well, yes beautiful, of course, but not only beautiful. She was a beam of light and energy, two things as absent from Agustín's life as Nature was from Polanco. The woman, who was in the middle of a work phone call, wore a beige skirt, a tucked-in white T-shirt printed with little blue and red squares, and white Italian sneakers. She had thick black eyebrows. Her skin, smooth and hydrated, seemed to be made of a different material than Agustín's.

The woman motioned to Agustín to place the tray with the three potted plants on the quarry tile floor and directed him to the living room to sit down. He obeyed. She sat on another couch and took a couple more minutes to finish her call.

It turned out she wasn't the client, but the client's friend. The client was rushing home from work and had asked her neighbor, the beam of light, to let Agustín into the apartment and entertain him while the client arrived with Agustín's money. The beam of light's name was Dora.

Once Agustín's nervousness waned a bit, he and Dora synched in a flowing conversation. They talked about everything, from traveling and movies to a recent high-profile murder and the upcoming elections, being interrupted every few minutes by Dora's work calls. The client was more than an hour late, but had it been up to Agustín, who normally hated tardiness, she would've taken longer. Before he left, he did something that would've seemed impossible when he first laid eyes on the beam of light: He asked for her number. She gave it to him. It all worked out.

"You're way out of my league," he'd say to her, both naked under her plush duvet, or while eating brunch on a Sunday. (Agustín didn't even really know what brunch was before Dora.)

"Don't say that," Dora would respond before kissing Agustín with those full lips that made him crazy.

But one afternoon—exactly six months, one week and five days after they met—she sat with him in her living room and, very calmly and respectfully, confessed that she'd met someone else. In fact, she'd been so respectful and calm that it didn't even occur to Agustín to get angry. He was paralyzed, sitting on a leather ottoman and staring at an antique glass-front cabinet that Dora had inherited from her aunt Roberta.

"See," said Agustín when he finally garnered the strength to talk, "I always said you were out of my league." This was part of the problem, he would later think. Agustín acted like a victim; Dora was a winner.

VELASCO

They continued to keep in touch. First, a text here, an email there. Then they'd call each other sporadically. It evolved into a friendship. They talked on the phone two, three, five times a week, sometimes every day. (She often referred her yuppie friends to his exotic plant business.) Sometimes she even called him at the exact moment he was thinking of her. Was this because they were connected telepathically or because he thought of her so often that the probability of her calling him while he thought of her was relatively high?

The day of the furniture call, for example, Agustín was watching news coverage of Paschalis while wondering what Dora would think of it. Paschalis was a dwarf planet that, on Thursday, would be the closest it had ever been to the Earth in hundreds of years and visible with the naked eye from certain parts of Latin America, including Mexico City. People were going crazy over it. What was up with this new planet no one had ever heard of? Conspiracy theories abounded: It was headed toward Earth; it would mess with our gravity; it was an alien spaceship disguised as a planet; and so on.

The news anchor, a man who looked more like a model than a journalist, was interviewing an exasperated woman with long, graying hair.

"Some say, doctor, that there will be a series of natural disasters on Thursday due to the proximity of this new planet—you seem to disagree."

"First of all," said the scientist, "I want to make it very clear that this is not a new planet. Paschalis is a dwarf planet, and we've known about its existence for almost two centuries."

Agustín wished Dora were next to him so he could rant to her about people's utter ignorance regarding anything scientific. He thought of calling her when his phone started vibrating. Magic!

"Welcome back," he said as a hello. Dora and the rich guy who had ripped her from Agustín's hands—Velasco was his name—had taken a cruise to the Netherlands, Belgium, the U.K. and the Frisian Islands, a trip that Agustín would maybe be able to afford after selling both his retinas.

"Right," said Dora. "Thank you."

"Have you seen all this Paschalis bullshit?"

"How are you?"

"Are you OK?" She wasn't being her usual, relaxed self. Most of their interactions were based on them joking around, they were almost never solemn, even when speaking of solemn matters.

"Do you need a couch?" she blurted.

"Are you with Velasco?"

"Two couches, actually. And a coffee table."

"That's all furniture Roberta gave you," he said.

"Exactly."

"He's right next to you, isn't he?"

"And?"

Velasco was already in his forties and probably wanted to marry Dora, start a family with her. Thinking about this made Agustín sick to his stomach.

"Call me later when we can talk freely," he told her.

LYDIA

Agustín was dating someone, by the way. Lydia. She was sweet. They had fun together, but there was no real substance to their relationship. He wasn't—knew he would never be—in love with her. Agustín thought they both knew it was a casual relationship until one night, walking down Álvaro Obregón from a dinner party, Lydia told him she loved him. Agustín was shocked. He panicked. He was also a bit stoned and drunk.

"I love you, too," he said.

And they kissed.

After the kiss, Lydia smiled and hugged him, resting her head on his torso as people passed them by on both sides and sirens wailed on a nearby street.

Now it was *I love you* when they spoke on the phone, *I love you* when they were falling asleep, *I love you* when they said good-bye. Agustín felt trapped. Was he supposed to tell her the truth, that he didn't, in fact, love her but would like to continue with their relationship because it made him fell less alone and distracted him from thinking about Dora so much?

WIDOW

Dora called the following morning while Agustín was on his way to deliver a red banana tree to a new client, a self-described widow.

"Am I on speakerphone?" she said. "You know I hate speakerphone."

"I'm driving. What was with you yesterday?"

"Oh, god. It's Velasco. He's been saying there are ghosts in the furniture ever since we came back from the cruise."

"Ghosts of your aunt? Can a dead person have more than one ghost?"

"Ghosts of us, Agustín. Of our relationship. He knows you practically lived here and that the furniture reminds me of you. He feels threatened by it."

Velasco felt threatened? Did that mean he had reason to feel threatened?

"That's ridiculous," he said.

"But what the hell, right? He promised to buy new furniture to replace it. So I obviously thought of you because your furniture is hideous. No offense."

"None taken."

"So?"

"Offer accepted."

"Great."

"From what I've seen of him on your Instagram, Velasco looks like a man of science, an inveterate materialist." Agustín was parking the truck just outside the widow's house in a posh suburb. "I guess I'll have to remember not to judge a book and so on." Everything was quiet there, except for the songs of birds and the sounds of servants sweeping driveways.

"You actually hit the nail on the head. He's an amateur astronomer. Or that's what he calls himself, anyway. This ghost thing is an aberration. I've actually never seen him more excited for anything than he is for Thursday."

"Paschalis?"

"We're having a big party on the roof of our building with some friends. Velasco's setting up his two super-expensive telescopes."

"Lydia and I will probably watch the thing on my laptop." Agustín said this because he felt like including his partner in the conversation was the right thing to do.

A white-haired man with a straw hat and a rag over his shoulder opened the door. He helped Agustín carry the red banana up the exterior brick steps. The widow, a big woman wearing a long-sleeve muumuu and smoking a cigarette, waited for him at the top.

Maybe it was because he had furniture on the brain, but he marveled at the exquisite decoration of the widow's house. Every sofa, chair and table looked heavy and well made. He regretted not charging her more for the red banana.

"The shovel's out back." She walked barefooted and Agustín followed her.

The woman's back yard had been turned into a minia-ture botanical garden—with carobs, white bark birches, and a small purple fountain tree. She had a whole section of carnivorous plants and rows of peanuts, cherry tomatoes, and basil.

"My husband's buried here," said the widow tapping the grass with her bare foot. "He's the one who feeds them."

Agustín started digging.

MOVERS

The following afternoon he returned home from work to find a moving truck parked outside his building. The moving men sat on the curb playing cards with bored expressions. As Agustín got out of his pickup truck, he heard a deep voice calling his name.

"You're finally here." Velasco was wearing a powder blue and maroon argyle sweater, gray slacks, and maroon penny loafers. "The guys were threatening to leave."

He was brawny, bald, and bearded, in contrast with Agustín who, at thirty-two, was still baby-faced and lanky.

Agustín purposely furrowed his brow in hopes of gaining some gravitas. He wiped his dirty palm on his T-shirt and stuck it out in front of him. "Nice to meet you." He felt as if he were introducing himself to a friend's dad.

"Yes," said his rival. "Thank you for this."

The sun was beginning to set.

"The only problem is," said Agustín, "all my old furniture is still up there."

"Dora told me you'd come to an agreement."

"We haven't agreed on a date."

"Well, buddy, I don't know what to tell you," he said motioning toward the movers.

"Where am I supposed to put all my other stuff?"

By the time the movers were done, the apartment looked as if the contents of two apartments were fighting each other. Or loving each other. His past mistakes wrestling his current life.

Whereas before there had only been one couch in the living room—a brown love seat, bought at discount, that was too small for him to lie down on—now said love seat was surrounded by a gray sectional with the softest of fabrics and two handwoven rattan chairs with loose cushions. (It was on that gray sectional that he'd first kissed Dora.) Agustín and Roberta's coffee tables were side to side, making it impossible for someone seated on the love seat, sectional, or rattan chairs to put their feet on the floor. The Hardy hibiscus had to be moved next to the window. To reach the recliner chair in the TV room, one now had to walk around an oak bookshelf in which Agustín would be finally able to put the botany books that at the moment were piled in three corners of his bedroom—the fourth corner belonging to a kaffir lily. Scattered around the apartment were loose ottomans, barstools, and a console table. Then, of course, there was the waist-high, glass-front antique cabinet. It stared at him. He hadn't thought of it when Dora offered him her furniture. Damn that thing. All it did was remind him of the shock of losing her. He carried it, it was heavy both in body and symbolism, and placed it near the entrance, next to the console table. He'd have to get rid of it.

The commotion of the movers after a long day of work left him exhausted. He stretched on his recliner with a beer in the armrest cup holder and turned on the news, a perfect antidote to a busy mind.

"Next up," said the anchorwoman with a bob, "Ariel-winning actress Crystal de la Orcana will tell us why she both fears and welcomes the approaching planet."

Agustín muted the television, closed his eyes and drifted to sleep.

GHOSTS

He was woken up by the words, *What the fuck?*

Dora was standing next to the bookshelf and she was mad. They must've gotten in a fight. He yawned as he tried to remember what it had been about. Bits of his dream leaked into his consciousness, making everything all the more confusing.

No, it wasn't Dora—it was Lydia. Of course. But she was standing next to Roberta's bookshelf. Now he remembered everything. It made him sad to still love Dora. Maybe he'd love her for the rest of his life.

"What's all this bullshit?"

It was Lydia who cursed like this. It was Lydia who wore clunky shoes to her office job.

"You went furniture shopping?" She hadn't figured out what was going on, but she knew it wasn't good.

"Dora." He said her name at the beginning, just to get it over with. "She gave me some of her aunt's furniture."

After a pause: "Why?"

It was Lydia whose eyes welled up when angry.

Agustín told her about Roberta and Velasco and the ghosts.

"So now you'll be living with the ghosts?"

Of course he would and that was the best, albeit bittersweet, thing about the whole arrangement—he'd be reminded, consciously and unconsciously, of the months he'd spent with Dora.

"Didn't you consider what I would think of this arrangement? What I will feel when I visit your apartment that's now full of her things?"

"Don't you think you might be exaggerating? It's just furniture."

Lydia stormed off to the bedroom and slammed the door behind her.

The news channel was playing a simulation of what would happen on Thursday. The enormous Earth, too big to fit in the picture, covered the bottom-left corner of the screen. Then, slowly, a smaller, texturized purple sphere began appearing in the top right-hand corner. In the background, outer space: dark, cold and supposedly infinite. It was like the dumb news channel was trying to tell him that, in the grand scheme of things, nothing meant anything. And yet everything felt like it meant so much.

ETHICS

Eventually Lydia calmed down and came back to the TV room. She sat on Agustín's lap and hugged him.

"I'm sorry," he said. "Should've told you about it."

Paschalis continued to dominate the news channel.

"Are you at all excited about this planet coming to visit us?" she said.

"I don't understand what the big deal is. I think people are just bored. You?"

Lydia shrugged. Agustín wondered about the moral ramifications of being with someone who loves you yet whom you don't love back and—more importantly—know you will never love. He cared for Lydia, sometimes deeply, but he knew what love felt like, and this wasn't it. He decided that it wasn't that bad as long as he didn't continue lying. He'd crossed a line by telling her he loved her. He wouldn't ever say those words to Lydia again. Next time she said them to him, regardless of the situation, he'd remain silent.

FRIENDSHIP

"What was I supposed to do?" said Dora, laughing. "I didn't know he was going to deliver them the next day. Our place is practically empty now. The rooms look so big."

"My apartment looks like a furniture store warehouse."

"Sorry." There was nothing sweeter than when Dora spoke with that repentant voice. "Was it awkward?"

"Picture me getting home from work to find your bearded beau standing next to my car, arms crossed over argyle like a member of a nerd street gang."

"Dear god with the argyle. He's crazy about it. Ridiculous."

She often criticized Velasco during their phone calls. Why? Did she really hate the argyle? Surely she loved it in some way and had told Velasco as much. Agustín pictured her in her apartment with nothing on except socks, underwear and an argyle sweater walking to the kitchen after a round of sex. Did she feel guilty about leaving him? Was their whole friendship predicated on her pity? Or was it the opposite? Was she trying to tell him something—something like, I'm here waiting for you. Come and get me.

"Does he know we talk on the phone?" Agustín immediately regretted asking this.

"Velasco?"

"Who else?"

"Does Lydia know we talk?"

Silence.

"Gotta go," she said. "Work stuff."

Agustín sat on the floor, next to the cabinet. He hated that cabinet, a souvenir of Dora's rejection. Would it be wrong to sell it? He could probably get a few thousand pesos for it. Nothing wrong with a few extra pesos and a little less sadness.

FLOOD

The city woke up early Thursday morning in a short but intense hailstorm. The public scientists had to work extra hard to reassure everyone that the weather had absolutely nothing to do with Paschalis' proximity.

On his drive to the shop, Agustín heard on the radio that the inhabitants of a fishing village in northwestern

Colombia had evacuated for fear of a tsunami. A famous Brazilian priest filled a soccer stadium in Fortaleza for a twelve-hour-long mass. For this special day, the motorcycle dealership next to Agustín's store had two women dancing outside in alien masks, bikini tops and booty shorts to reggaeton blasting from a subwoofer.

Once inside, his mind was forced to other, more immediate things. A humidifier in the tropical plant section had broken overnight, causing minor flooding.

After mopping it all up, Agustín checked that the bleeding heart vine, among the most capricious of tropical flowers, had not been affected by the shift in humidity. Then he spoke on the phone with the repairman while spraying water on the petals of the flamingo and temple flowers.

His phone rang at noon. It was the widow.

"*Pseudobombax ellipticum,*" she said in a hoarse voice. Rich widows wake up late. "I need three."

The blossom of the shaving bush tree, as that plant was commonly known, was one of Agustín's favorites: pink and spiky, wild in an elegant way. It almost looked like flora from another planet, maybe even a dwarf planet.

"I only have one in stock," he said. "But if you give me a week or two—."

"I need you to plant three *Pseudobombax elliptica* tonight at nine fifty-two p.m."

"I could call around, but I would be very surprised if—."

"One will suffice," said the widow. Then she hung up.

DENIAL

"What precautions would you recommend people take tonight?" said the cable news host.

This scientist was in his university office, index finger to earpiece. "I must have not explained myself correctly."

"You have, doctor. But I'm sure not even someone like you could deny the *possibility*—."

"I would recommend people take no precautions. No precautions at all. Apart from the normal precautions they take on any given day. Look both ways before crossing the street, for example. Don't eat too much sugar."

Agustín walked around the bookshelf to the hallway and into the kitchen. He sat at the wooden table to eat an apple and manchego while he did some bookkeeping on his laptop.

Lydia called: "I think we should do something tonight."

"Why?"

"Are you angry?"

"Just tell me what you want to do tonight."

"Everyone's celebrating Paschalis. Don't you want to come over? Or we could go to Marcela's. She's having a party."

"There's nothing to celebrate." He realized he sounded like a teenager arguing with his mother about Christmas dinner with the family. "Besides, I have to work."

She asked again if something was the matter. He said no and they ended the call. No I love you this time.

Agustín looked at the cabinet and thought of the widow. Of course! It would fit perfectly in her home.

And he wouldn't try to sell it to her, either. He'd just tell her he'd inherited from an aunt but had no place for it. Then the cabinet would be gone from his life forever.

TIME

"It came to me in a dream," said the widow as Agustín and the man with the straw hat placed the shaving bush next to the Indonesian wax ginger.

The man with the straw hat excused himself. Did he live here in some sort of service quarters? Had the man with the straw hat met the man resting underneath the garden? How long ago had the husband died?

The widow continued: "In this dream, a South African golden mole instructed me to plant three *Pseudobombax elliptica* at the moment of Earth's most intense proximity to Paschalis. I imagine the mole represented my husband, though that might be too obvious."

Agustín stabbed the ground with the shovel and began digging.

"I didn't know of the existence of this plant before the dream, much less its scientific name," said the widow. "How do you explain that?"

Agustín had had it with all this mystical bullshit regarding magical planets and ghosts. "I guess I can't," he said as he continued to dig, without looking up.

The widow looked intently at the screen of her phone, waiting for the right moment to plant the shaving bush tree. Every so often she'd look up at Paschalis, which would appear, so said the news channel, much larger than the largest star.

After he finished digging the hole, Agustín removed the plant from its plastic pot. The thin roots seemed to stretch in excitement.

"Now!" said the widow. And in went the bush tree, followed by dirt. "Look!" she said. "Look at Paschalis! It's majestic!"

Agustín just stood there, arms akimbo, looking down. He refused to participate in such madness, even at the request of a client.

The widow stared at the night sky, taking it all in. Then she pulled out a check folded in half from her breast pocket and handed it to Agustín. He thanked her as he put the check in his jacket pocket.

The man with the straw hat was nowhere to be seen, so Agustín let himself out. It wasn't until he'd closed the door that he saw the cabinet—covered in blankets that were fastened with rope—sticking out of the bed of his pickup truck, taunting him.

The idea of ringing the doorbell and going back in and explaining to the widow that he had a free antique cabinet for her seemed ridiculous now. He could, however, leave the thing outside the widow's door. She'd probably think it was a gift from her husband.

Agustín climbed on to the bed of the truck and unwrapped the blankets. Dora's rejection rose from the cabinet like steam. Agustín realized that the love of his life would most certainly marry Velasco. Maybe not this year, but probably the next. They'd be together forever. They would have children, and their children would have strange names and dress in fine clothing. He saw them, all four of them: Dora, Velasco, and the two handsome boys standing together for a picture. He saw Lydia meeting a man at Marcela's party and realizing that Agustín didn't love her.

Another realization: It was easier to get the cabinet on the truck than off of it. There was no way he'd be able to get it down without the help of the man with the straw hat.

So he dropped it. Or he threw it down. The thing smashed to pieces. It made a nasty sound, like a car wreck. Shards of thick glass and wood were everywhere. It was on a piece of glass, on an empty street among so much exotic silence, that Agustín saw the reflection of Paschalis. The planet was looking down at him.

UNHAPPINESS, GUANAJUATO

ALSO KNOWN AS RUMINATION.

As much as it might seem incredible to someone like you or me, happiness, wait, Happiness, hasn't always had a positive connotation for everyone. This will be easier to accept if you consider that no one thing has been anything, always, for everyone. Most things have been many things for at least some people. Nothing has at times meant Everything and at others meant Some Things. For long stretches of time Nothing actually meant nothing. But I must stop myself because I have the tendency to spin uncontrollably into spirals of confusion and—sometimes—complete nonsense.

FOR EXAMPLE: MADDEN'S SAVAGES.

The first records of a society that considered Happiness to be something to avoid rather than the Ultimate Goal come from Scottish anthropologist Newman J. Madden. When he died in 1809, Dr. Madden was working on a book about a tribe, which he simply referred to as the Savages, dwellers of a village near what today is Alice Springs, Australia, people who associated Happiness with death and decay. "We are born crying," wrote Dr. Madden, "and die, when we die as nature intended us to, with a lazy smile on our faces, so it shouldn't be surprising that the Savages think of bursts of happiness as little pushes and shoves towards nonexistence."

The manuscript goes on to explain a ritual wherein Madden's Savages—which some modern anthropologists think might be an offshoot of the Noogri tribe—slashed their infants' cheeks as a rite of passage, rendering them forever incapable of smiling. (Portraits of the brutally scarred faces of Madden's Savages can be found among the anthropologist's papers at the University of California, Berkeley.)

THE FALSE REASON WHY I'M TELLING THIS STORY: A SMOKE SCREEN.

Then there was, of course, the Sorg (Grief) cult in Stockholm during the late nineteenth century. Its members would go years without being exposed to sunlight, but the group was dismantled after their unsuccessful attempt to assassinate Sofia of Nassau. During America's Great Depression something called the Frown Militia, a gang of ultra-right-wing manic-depressives who wanted to take over the country, appeared and quickly disappeared in Oklahoma.* But much has already been written about these and other cases of note. Besides, I am not an anthropologist; nor did I ever finish medical school. The only reason I feel compelled to write this is that my grandfather died last week. He himself once belonged to what in academic circles are known as societies of unhappiness.

Unlike what most people think and common sense suggests, the Frown Militia got its name not from the facial gesture associated with being sad, but rather from its founder Wallace T. Frown.

THE SOCIETY.

You can call it a cult, commune, or whatever else provides you with a better understanding of the phenomenon. I call it a society. All they wanted was a paradigm shift that would better suit their reality. I've heard of worse things.

Dr. Blanco's society of unhappiness might be the most recent one on record. From the very little that has been written of it, it's still unclear if it was founded in 1946 or 1949. My grandparents Tomás and Mariana didn't join until the winter of '51.

TOMÁS.

The youngest child of one of Mexico City's most prominent families, at thirty Tomás de Feo had already built a name for himself as a lawyer and a professor, even serving as a trusted legal advisor to President Miguel Alemán. Alemán, as Mexico's sitting mandatary, officiated Tomás' marriage to Mariana Schiffner, a beautiful young woman who'd turned sixteen only a month before the wedding.

There's a slight mention of my grandfather in Alemán's colossal and self-serving autobiography. After dedicating a single paragraph to Tomás' rise and fall, Alemán concludes that "Licenciado de Feo was a man whose genius sadly morphed into complete lunacy."

HIS MIND WAS ALL ANYONE SPOKE OF.

Mariana's father, my great-grandfather Knut, described Tomás in his diaries as "an ambitious man with rare intelligence who, nonetheless, seems to know nothing of what the joys of life can bring. Most of the time he's deep in thought, and what he seems to be thinking about is DEATH."

THE MIRALARGA EPISODE.

Not long after the wedding, there was an episode in which Tomás refused to leave his office on the thirty-second floor of the Torre Miralarga for over seventy-five hours. After finally stumbling out into the hallway, the young lawyer adamantly refused to be institutionalized and was back to work the following week.

MAJOR DEPRESSIVE DISORDER.

I understand perfectly what Tomás was going through because his nasty melancholic gene squeezed its way into my father's bloodstream and then skipped onto my brother Javier's and mine. It must be said at some point, it might as well be here, that my father, Jerónimo de Feo, hanged himself one night from the thick branches of a coral tree in the courtyard of his law firm in downtown Mexico City.

XX.

My sister, Tamara, I'm proud to report, seems to be free of the disease. She lives in Cambridge, Massachusetts, with her husband and four children.

THREE NUNS WALK INTO A HOSPITAL ROOM.

So yes, Tomás de Feo was a dark cloud of a man, but for a large part of his life he, like everyone else, was obsessed with finding Happiness. From a very early age he read the great philosophers and left dozens of notebooks filled with scribbled notes of his reactions. I've read hundreds of pages from his notebooks and must say that it's painful to trace the mental footsteps of a man who is so clearly not in control of his spirit. One day he'd write something like, "Happiness is understanding that we are everything, everything is us." Then, after twenty pages filled with minuscule scribbling, he'd come to the conclusion that "to be truly content one must accept that he is nothing. We don't exist."

Tomás attended seminars on Happiness, made at least five trips to Boston to visit one of the psychiatrists who was working to include Major Depression in the first version of the DSM, escaped to Buddhist retreats, and even dabbled with hallucinogenics. Nothing worked.

Finally, in 1952, frustrated by the only problem that his brain couldn't seem to resolve—for it was a problem of the brain itself—Tomás tried to take his life by ingesting a cocktail of sleeping pills and rat poison. It was a miracle, or at least that's what most would call it, that

Mariana felt ill while at a visit to her sister's and decided to return home early that day. So it was that Tomás awoke in the Hospital Católico with three nuns praying at his bedside and Mariana weeping behind them.

LEMMINGS.

Not long after his botched suicide attempt, Tomás published an essay in *El Universal*'s culture supplement titled "On Escaping Melancholia." The essay, which catalogued my grandfather's search for Happiness, was widely read in Mexico, and a French translation even made it to the pages of *Le Monde*. As a result, my grandfather received dozens of letters from the depressed and their close ones thanking him for raising consciousness about the disease.

Then one day he opened a letter from Dr. Efraín Blanco. Dr. Blanco's missive was aggressive and condescending. Tomás, according to Dr. Blanco, had been doing it all wrong. "Sadness is Man's natural state," reads Dr. Blanco's beautiful handwriting. "Escaping melancholia is as unnatural as fasting or chastity. It is Culture along with the powers that be who have convinced us that smiling, which, as everyone knows, not only feels but also looks unnatural, is the face's most positive expression. Chasing Culture's promise of Happiness—a mirage, at best—is as ludicrous and destined to failure as those imbecile rodents who follow each other off a cliff."*

*Dr. Blanco was, no doubt, referring to the popular (and completely false) myth that at a certain age lemmings commit suicide by jumping off a cliff.

THE ROAD TO UNHAPPINESS.

It is unclear why Tomás and Mariana got in their Chrysler Town & Country and drove to see Dr. Blanco that October day. Half my family argues that Tomás, who was also known for his sudden bursts of uncontrollable rage, had his revolver with him and was planning to kill the only person who had ever dared to call him obtuse. The other half of the de Feos argues that he just wanted to talk with the man. After all, why would he have taken his wife on a road trip just to witness a murder?

I've driven that road that my grandfather took to Guanajuato many times, because as a student I did my residency in León, the state's most important city. After a few weeks of commuting, I decided that in one of those drives to Guanajuato I'd detour to Dr. Blanco's estate. Young and brazen, I began asking around in de Feo family events if anyone knew exactly where the estate was located. My family spoke about the society frequently, but they always did so in vague terms, never providing anything as specific as location. All I could find out was that it was a few kilometers from a little village called Loma Escondida.

I drove toward the general area, and once I got close enough to Loma Escondida, I began to ask the locals for directions. Everyone looked at me like I was asking them if they knew which road to take to El Dorado. "Doctor who?" they said. "Never heard of him." As I was about to give up my search for the estate I pulled into a gas station to buy some snacks and asked the cashier, a good-humored old man, if he knew how to get to where I wanted to go. He laughed. "Tristeza?" I was confused. "Nobody knows about that place anymore," he said, "but we used to call it Tristeza."*

Tristeza was a ghost town. Its cement, unpainted villas were falling apart and the paint of the black mansion where Dr. Blanco once lived with his three wives and dozen children was fading. I didn't stay long. My companion felt scared and uneasy and begged me to take her away from Tristeza. I don't blame her. The town's all around vibe—a term I stay away from—was unsettling.

I often try to imagine what Tristeza looked like when Tomás and Mariana arrived that afternoon in the autumn of 1952. Sure, the villas and the mansion were terribly depressing even then—I've heard that all furniture, clothes, and belongings had to be painted black—but there were broccoli and strawberry plantations that must've looked beautiful even amid so much gloom.

Dr. Blanco, who was by all accounts an incredibly charming man, must've made some impression on Tomás, because that night he and Mariana drove back to Mexico City, packed their bags and drove right back to Tristeza. A cement hut only a few meters from the black mansion welcomed them.

*Unhappiness

FINDINGS.

Some have suggested that Dr. Blanco wasn't even a real doctor, but rather a classic example of the charismatic and psychopathic leader who in this case found a "cause" that just happened to be psychiatric in nature. False. Dr. Blanco was, at one point, a real psychiatrist.

The only real investigative work I've done regarding Tristeza has been to look up Dr. Blanco's records in the Mexican Psychiatric Association (AMP). Here are my findings:

Elías Blanco arrived at the Washington University School of Medicine in Saint Louis in 1926. No one, at least no one that I know of, knows anything about him before then. In 1932 Dr. Blanco arrived in Mexico City, where he started his practice. In 1936 he had his license taken away for what the AMP called "improper use of medication" and "multiple violations of AMP stipulations." At some point during the next couple of years, he moved to Guanajuato with a dozen or so of his patients. One of those original settlers of Tristeza was Diana Velasco-Cabañero, co-heir to the fortune of railroad tycoon Alonso Velasco-Cabañero. Diana would later become one of Dr. Blanco's wives and give birth to two of his children.

MR. VACA.

It seems logical to think that those first settlers of Tristeza were all either depressives or bipolar, though that very well may not be the case. As I've said repeatedly, not much is known about Dr. Blanco's society. That everyone wore black we know because there exist, amid Dr. Blanco's papers in the library of the Universidad

Nacional, two hazy pictures of Tristeza taken from above, maybe from a tree, maybe from an actual observation tower that was later destroyed.

Happiness was outlawed in Tristeza. We know from a rare letter to his family. one that Guillermo Vaca snuck out to the post office, that if someone was deemed to be happy they would immediately be put away in a small cement hut with no windows and a narrow steel door.*

According to Mr. Vaca, the hardest thing about living in Tristeza was staying productive while being sad. Dr. Blanco was, after all, delivering kilos and kilos of strawberries and broccoli to León on a regular basis, and someone had to do the picking. In his letter, Mr. Vaca tells of people working on the field breaking down in crying fits or suddenly falling asleep.

Mr. Vaca, who was once rescued from the ledge of a twenty-story office building, was not complaining about Dr. Blanco's policies, just describing them.

SEX IN TRISTEZA.

Have I wondered if Mariana was one of Dr. Blanco's lovers? Of course I have. She was a very beautiful, very young woman. (The leader liked them young.) Meanwhile, Dr. Blanco was a middle-aged man of short stature and a pencil-thin mustache. Some people say that the only reason he began the society was so he could have access to women that would, in a regular environment, not even give him the light of day. I am not one of those people.

FOOD IN TRISTEZA.

The inhabitants of Tristeza didn't eat the strawberries and vegetables they grew. In fact, they didn't eat fruits and vegetables at all. Dr. Blanco, who was an iconoclast if he was anything, thought that we only have positive ideas about those foods because they make us feel "good." Also prohibited in Tristeza were foods rich in carbohydrates. A normal lunch in the society would consist of pork, fried eggs, wine and coffee. "We consume foods that make us sluggish," said Dr. Blanco in a rare letter to one of his close friends from St. Louis. "Sluggishness leads to discomfort, irritability, and sedentariousness (sic), which in turn lead to questioning and contemplation." Exercise, except in the form of sex, was also prohibited in Tristeza.

DREAMS.

I often dream of Tristeza. In some of these dreams I am Dr. Blanco, while in others I am my grandfather, myself, or an anonymous member of the society. There are some dreams in which I am God, looking down on Tristeza through the clouds. Mostly, these dreams cause me anxiety and stress, but sometimes they fill me with serenity. There is a recurring dream in which I am riding a goat in a never-ending strawberry field and the goat slowly dies. Interpret that if you like, but I find that the more I study dreams the more meaningless they become. That might be true for everything under Reality.

I also daydream about Tristeza. (I am certain that adult daydreaming is a sign of stunted maturity.) When

I had a job I'd spent most of my time in the office thinking about the society. Now, unemployed, a dweller in the big house my mother left me, I spend afternoons in her old room scratching my rough cheeks and pretending I am an inhabitant of Tristeza or nursing the fantasy that I am a high-ranking member of the government's secret police sent along with a team of soldiers to shut the society down. For a long time it shamed me how often I thought of Dr. Blanco fucking this or that wife in the bedroom, the kitchen, the living room. The thought of him in bed with young Mariana often enters my head, and I've stopped trying to push it out. It must be there for a reason. I like to picture Tristeza's inhabitants, clad in black, mumbling and grumbling, cursing this and that, feeling at the same time alone and part of something. It is, I guess, a collective loneliness, which is as good a loneliness as there is.

STANCE.

It's hard for a man of my age and circumstance to take a stance on anything, much less on something as hazy and personal as Tristeza, Guanajuato. At times I think that living there would've worked for me, whatever that may mean. I've felt the taunting tyranny of the Happiness bait since I can remember. Maybe Dr. Blanco would've allowed me to escape from it. There wasn't a single suicide that I know of in Tristeza, a place whose dwellers were mostly prone to suicide. That puts a bitter smile on my face.

MY MOTHER SLEPT CALMLY IN HER CRIB.

Not to say that Dr. Blanco wasn't a charlatan. In 1957 he took all the broccoli and strawberry money and disappeared forever with a Tristeza newcomer. But aren't all leaders charlatans? If they're not fooling us they're fooling themselves. (And when they find out they've been fooling themselves they go on to fool us.)

Tomás and Mariana stayed in Tristeza for a few months after Dr. Blanco's departure in hopes of saving the society. In fact, my uncle Ernesto was born in post-Dr. Blanco Tristeza. But the new leadership failed. All hope had left with the money. My grandparents returned to Mexico City in 1958, and in 1962, driving back from a party, Tomás shot Mariana in the temple and then drove off a cliff.

THE REAL REASON I AM TELLING THIS STORY.

I, of course, would've never had a child on purpose. I hope not to sound too drenched in self-pity when I say that I am well aware of the black stain that runs through my genetic material. But, alas, it happened.

A few weeks after my forty-first birthday I received a call from Teresa Alba, a beautiful Nicaraguan graduate student who had come to Mexico for a conference and whom I met at the lobby bar of a hotel. She asked me if I remembered her. Of course I did. I hadn't slept with a woman for years before I slept with Teresa and hadn't slept with one since.

"I—we had a son," she said.

My knees buckled. My throat went dry. I remember grabbing on to a large portrait of one of my aunts that decorated my bedroom wall. "Excuse me?"

Silence.

"Are you sure?"

"He's three months old," she said. "If I remember your face correctly the little

guy looks just like his father."

"How did you get my number?"

"I wasn't even going to tell you, Joaquín. I guess I'm not as cruel as I thought."

I suggested that maybe she was crueler. I was angry at myself, which means I was angry at the world.

ACKNOWLEDGEMENTS.

I met little Octavio in the Managua airport a couple of days after the phone call. He was sleeping in his mother's arms. Next to Teresa stood her newfound boyfriend, a young poet with a kind smile and a high-pitched voice.

I'd like to say that holding Octavio cured me, saved me, but the truth is that it only made things worse. As I paced back and forth in Teresa's house with my son in my arms, I could see it in his eyes, the disease, the lifetime of—.

I'll stop here. I don't even know if I want him to read this. But maybe it will help him hate me instead of himself.

THE WORST THING ABOUT
HAVING SEX WITH ME

I waited for her outside an old, powder-blue building near my place that looked like it would fall in the next earthquake. Inside lived and worked a popular Korean hair stylist and her family. This was back when poor immigrant stylists were all the rage among rich Mexican women. *I found the best one! She's a fat Moldovan who shares a one-bedroom with her in-laws.*

It was dark and beginning to rain when Aitana stepped out of the graffitied door. Her hair looked prettier, though not necessarily shorter. It struck me as odd that she wasn't all in black. (I, not being Catholic and afraid of offending someone, had draped myself in that color from my sweater down to my shoes.) She carried the same oversized hand-bag, almost a diaper bag, which she had brought on our other dates.

Aitana looked sad as hell, as if she'd cried every day ever since she'd popped out of her mother more than three decades ago. She asked me to drive because she said she'd been driving all day and was sick of it.

I tried to make small talk as we chopped through traffic, and she did her best to play along. Every so often one of her friends would call her freaking out re: the people out in the streets protesting the killing of a Oaxacan family (kids included) by the army. Or were they protesting the dozens of students jailed for no reason? Hopefully they wouldn't affect the area near the church.

She smiled as we exited the Viaducto to get onto Periférico. "I bet you've never had a fourth date at a funeral."

"I'd rather this than a wedding," I said.

"You're joking."

"I hate dancing. Other people dancing, me dancing, the idea of dancing."

This made her laugh.

We'd met online and set our first rendezvous at a bookstore in Polanco. She'd spent the previous night at the hospital with Ángeles, a friend of hers who was sick, and so had arrived with dark bags under her eyes. She yawned when I asked her if she wanted to go to a bar, so we decided instead on a pizza place. It wasn't a good first date by any stretch—she being so nervous, tired, and worried about her friend, while I was just as nervous plus unsure if she was just exaggerating her tiredness as an excuse to escape the date early. Yet when the evening was coming to a close, as I walked her to her car, something changed. It was probably just that we relaxed a bit. And so we decided to see each other the following Friday. Then again the following Tuesday, which led to plans to meet again on Thursday.

Then Ángeles died.

Aitana called me weeping, distraught.

Of course I found it a bit odd that this woman whom I barely knew was leaning on me during such a tragic event in her life, but who was I kidding? We were both lonely people desperately trying to be less lonely. With that in mind, it was the most normal thing in the world. Also, odd or not, all I could really do was comfort her.

"So I won't be able to make it on Thursday."

"Don't even worry about that."

"They're having the funeral that day."

"We'll get coffee when you feel better."

"Unless you want to come with me to the funeral."

"Oh. Well. I mean. If you …."

Driving on the Periférico I asked her to tell me again the name of the church.

"Medugorje."

"My mom's house is on the way," I said in what could almost be described as a bubbly tone. "I'll get to show you where I grew up." It shames me to admit this, but I wanted her to know that even though times were tough for me, I'd grown up like her, in a nice house nested inside a wealthy neighborhood.

"Actually," she said, "would you mind if we stopped there for a second so I can change?"

"You brought clothes?"

She pointed to her bag. "I was going to have you stop at Starbucks or something."

Dread rose from my lower abdomen, expanding into my chest.

"Or we can still just go to a Starbucks."

"No. It's fine." I regretted these words immediately. Why didn't I make up some excuse? Could've just told her the truth, that my mom had recently had eye surgery and it would be awkward to bring a date over. Or the other, more important, truth, that it's always been a huge deal for me to introduce my mom to someone I'm dating because, although she's a perfectly nice woman, in private she's nosy and judgmental. That it's only happened twice, with longtime girlfriends. That I like to keep my compartments compartmentalized. That it was never easy being her son.

Then I realized there was no reason they actually had to meet. My mom, blinded by gauze, was probably upstairs in her bedroom.

We drove by my school; the park where I played countless hours of soccer and basketball; the convenience store where, at fourteen, I purchased my first pack of Camels; the house where I clumsily lost my virginity; my grandparents' (R.I.P.) house.

Luz, my mother's live-in maid for the past fifteen years, opened the back door. She looked surprised that I'd brought someone over.

I sneaked my date into the downstairs bathroom trying to act calmly, speaking in a low voice yet not in a whisper. Aitana plucked a makeup kit from her bag.

"I'm going upstairs to say hi to my mom."

It was always comforting yet sad to be back there. Too much safety, too many bad memories.

Her excited smile was the first thing I saw as I opened the door. The TV was tuned to a news channel covering the day's protests. The two giant gauze eyepatches made my mom look like an insect. She was lying in bed, under her fluffy, white duvet, pillows propped up behind her.

"How did you know it was me?"

"I heard you coming up the stairs," she said. "I know your rhythms."

My mom doesn't know everything about me, but she knows a lot and thinks she knows it all.

I sat on the white couch, which faced the room as a whole. The TV images were familiar: things broken, torndown, set aflame. "I brought a friend. She needed to use the bathroom. We'll be leaving in a sec."

My mom, for my sake, didn't react to this in any way.

I asked her how she was doing.

"I'm sick of these damn things," she said, obviously referring to the patches. "Can't do anything but listen to music or the news. And the news is so depressing. Won't see the doctor until next week. I talked to him yesterday, and he said everything's fine. Right. For him everything's always fine. I've become convinced that sight is the most important of the senses. I can't read, watch movies, drive … I'm trapped inside my head."

My mom's always been completely incapable of reacting to a situation with anything that even resembles objectivity. She would've had the same opinion of any other sense she temporarily lost.

"Rita called me," she said with fake nonchalance.

"Or you called her."

"She called me."

"Mom, please don't. You know how this upsets me."

"Can I just relay to you what she told me? Then you're free to act as you please."

After the magazine for which I wrote crumbled, I'd been unemployed for almost a year. The situation had me worried, though maybe not as worried as I should have been. On the other hand, my mom was terrified for my future. She'd been pestering her friends to get their husbands to help me find a job and present it to me as if her friends' husbands were just dying, for no reason at all, to get me hired. It was humiliating.

"I know what you're going to say she told you."

"She was talking to Marco about you and he thought you sounded like such an interesting guy. He said, 'I'd love to pick his brain.' Those were his words."

"Right. A savvy businessman wants to pick my brain. I don't see anything strange with that."

"Why don't you just meet with him for coffee? You have nothing to lose."

The thing was I had—before catching on to what my mom was up to—met with some of her friends' husbands. They were very nice to me, just like their wives had ordered them to be, and nothing ever came to anything. I was unemployable. Again, humiliating.

A slight knock on the ajar door made me realize I knew Luz's rhythms, as it was immediately clear to me it wasn't her.

Aitana walked in. She was all in black, holding one of those Chanel makeup squares in one hand and her bag in the other.

Seeing her there made me feel like my stomach was about to implode. This was my mother's room. Our sanctum. When I still lived with her, and I lived with her far too long, her room was where I'd go on and on about my (and the world's) troubles, where she would listen for as long as I needed her to.

My mom muted the TV and turned her face to Aitana as if she could see her.

"Sorry, ma'am," said Aitana. "I was downstairs debating if it was ruder to not say hello to you or to come up uninvited."

"Oh please, dear. You did the right thing."

Aitana closed the door and introduced herself as she sat next to me. "So sorry. Had I known you were indisposed …."

"I needed company anyway. I'm going crazy in this room all by myself."

In a lot of ways, maybe even in most ways, Aitana had more in common with my mom than with me: Their upper-crust way of talking, their centrist political views, the subtle social conventions, and so on. I felt like they'd communicated with each other way more than I was able to pick up. Had my mom already figured her—and thus me—out?

I explained to Aitana the ins and outs of my mother's surgery. She listened attentively and wished her the best.

"We're off," I said, relieved that finally the whole thing was coming to an end. "I'll call you later."

"We don't mean to be rude, ma'am, but I'm sure Jero told you about the situation."

"He was just starting to." My mom loved an excuse to lie, especially if that excuse was helping her son out in some way.

"A very dear friend of mine died of cancer this week."

Aitana's eyes got watery. I handed her a box of tissues from my mother's bedside table.

"I'm so sorry to hear that."

"She was very sick for very long. It was hell for her family." The word hell comes out differently when it's said by someone who, like Aitana, had a big, gold Virgin of Guadalupe medallion hanging from her neck. "She left two little sons."

My mother cringed. "So you're going to the funeral."

"At Our Lady of Medugorje."

"The one near the yellow bridge?"

"Yes."

"But you'll never make it," she said this to me. "Not tonight. Not from here." My mom turned the volume back up. "Reforma's closed."

It's natural for people to place social unrest they see on TV on a land far away and/or in another time, but the violence was happening all around us, right at that moment. We were trapped by it. Looking closer I recognized the houses, the stoplights, the businesses.

Aitana's phone vibrated and lit up as she took it out of her bag. "Oh no. I always forget to check my phone. It's been cancelled." She dried the tears from her face with a tissue.

I felt shame for the relief that swept over me now that I wouldn't have to attend the funeral. The more time I spent with Aitana, the clearer it was to me that nothing would come of it. All I hoped now was that the protests died down soon so we could get out of there and I could be alone again, free, in my apartment.

A bus was set on fire; the police shot tear gas canisters.

"I can't figure out if this country's finally escaping its past or backing itself into a corner," said my mom.

"Maybe that's why they call it a Mexican standoff."

"A what?" said Aitana.

"When two or more people are pointing a gun at each other, Americans call it a Mexican standoff. Maybe it's three or more. No one has the advantage and no one has a logical way out of the situation. Like that great, super-long bar scene in *Inglorious Basterds*."

"I don't think I saw that?"

Why did I think nothing would come of it? First of all, Aitana, like me, was a sad person, and it's always scared me to pair up with a fellow sad person. Even worse than just sad, she seemed resigned. "Some people are born angry," she'd said to me on our second date. It was fine by her that life would be kind of miserable and uneventful.

Then there was the sex.

The third date was a movie at my place. She began taking her clothes off as soon as we kissed, which is neither a good nor a bad thing but, for reasons which we'll get to later, a bit too fast for this shy loser. I'm in no hurry, I told her. She said OK, but then more clothes were released and she again insisted. Then insisted some more and then some more until I finally had to step out of the room in my underwear.

The whole experience, her neediness, or maybe the fact that she wanted me, was a big turnoff.

And finally, what kind of person doesn't know if they've seen *Inglorious Basterds*?

"I'm optimistic," I said. "Mexico's bleeding its worst diseases out. Sure, it's a gruesome sight, but unfortunately I don't think there was any other way."

"It's worse than ever," said Aitana. "Terrifying."

"Horrible!" said my mom in a high-pitched tone. "I'm trapped here. All I can do is listen to the news all day, and it's making me very depressed. Very depressed. You should get back into comedy. More than ever this country needs to laugh."

"Comedy?" said Aitana. "You're a comedian?"

"Was."

"When?"

"For a couple of years after university."

"You don't know about his comedy career?"

"I don't think anyone but my mom would call it a career."

"How long have you two known each other?"

"This is our fourth date," said Aitana. "Imagine that: a fourth date and we were going to a funeral."

"My fourth date with his dad was to a movie and the film caught on fire. Should've been a sign."

"Come on, you do not remember your fourth date with my dad."

"You don't tell me what I do and don't remember! I'm blind, not dumb!"

It wasn't really until then, when I heard her come after me like that in self-defense, that I realized how hard this surgery had been for her. My mom, always effusive about the (often absurd) worries and anxieties she has regarding other people's lives, never shows distress about her own.

Her father and both her father's parents had gone blind. Now she'd submitted herself to an experimental (and very aggressive) surgery to delay her own blindness. Of course she was going insane, unable to do anything without assistance, haunted every waking hour by her own mortality.

Thinking this, I started going a bit crazy myself. What if the surgery didn't work? What if when I grew old there was still nothing that worked? How would I survive? At least my mom had a comfortable house, money. She had Luz, my sister, and me. I would have nothing and no one. It was such a terrible future I couldn't even imagine it. Maybe I was going crazy in my own, lazy way. This was a craziness that stilted me, made me an observer of life instead of a participant in it.

"Why'd you quit comedy?"

"I stunk."

"He was great. Had he stuck with it, by now …."

"Mom."

"… he'd probably be …."

"Mom. You never even saw me."

"You wouldn't let me! Besides, Rebecca said …."

"You didn't let your own mom come to a show?"

"Why would I want her to come?" Now I was angry at both of them. "Half the act was about her!"

"Jerónimo!" said Aitana in a chiding/offended voice that reminded me of you-know-who.

"Mexicans," I pontificated, "have a pathological view on family."

"You're Mexican, too," said my mother.

"Not in that sense."

It had all escalated so quickly. It always does when I'm with my mom. We start out friendly—courteous, even—and suddenly all the complicated feelings we have toward each other bubble up. She wakes up the snotty teenager living inside me.

"This country took in all four of your grandparents."

"This country's shit," I said, contradicting my earlier assertions about the bleeding out and whatnot. "Just look at what's going on. One can't even go on a nice date to a funeral."

The joke got no response.

As the city went up in flames, like it had so many times before, I wondered how we were ever going to leave my mom's house. If the protests went late into the night, would my date invite herself to stay overnight? If she didn't, my mom would surely bring it up, thinking it rude not to.

"Aitana," said my mother, hand on her forehead, "I didn't even ask you if you wanted some coffee or something." She dialed Luz's number. (Before cell phones, both women communicated by shouting.) "Luz, please bring up …."

"Green tea," said Aitana. "Thank you."

"A green tea. And for Jero …."

"I'm fine."

"A coffee. Decaf. I'll have a Diet Coke."

"It was actually the reason I stopped," I said to Aitana. "Besides lack of talent."

"What was?"

"The chunk about my mom."

"Can you stop it with that?"

"Oh, dear," said my mom. "I've heard all about it. Really, it's OK."

"I had these jokes about our relationship. Good jokes. I would say the half of my act that dealt with her was the better half."

"And?"

"Audiences didn't seem to agree. They invariably sided with her. The jokes don't work if they take her side. So I made them meaner hoping they would get the point."

Aitana was disappointed in me.

"They didn't, which, in turn, made me very depressed. What had drawn me into comedy in the first place was feeling misunderstood, but then I just became a misunderstood comedian."

The truth was my act didn't turn meaner, but sadder. I lied for my mom's sake. Things were sad enough already.

There was, for example, this story about my third-grade essay. We were a couple of years into the divorce. I remember not being able to sleep and having terrible headaches. One evening my mom called me into her room. She cried holding a sheet of notebook paper. I asked her what the matter was. "Is this what you want?" she said to me. I remember it as if it were happening at this moment. She had read a homework assignment I'd written titled, "My Parents," in which I described my mom and dad, except that instead of describing my actual mom I'd written about my father's mistress-turned-wife. Adding to the confusion, I had no memory of writing "My Parents."

Obviously, jokes were woven into the essay story, but I was still too angry at my mom, too sad for that eight-year-old boy, to convey anything but anger and sadness. Writing this I still get the urge to time-travel back to that moment and ask my mom how she has the metaphorical balls to ask that question to a kid who's still shaken up by his parents' violent separation.

"What about the other half?"

"Huh?"

"Of your act."

My mom jumped in. "It was great. It was all great!"

"Mom!"

"She asked!"

"It was self-deprecating and got more laughs."

"What was it about?"

"All types of stuff."

"Do a bit for us."

Just how high was Aitana's threshold for awkwardness?

"I will definitely not do a bit for you and my mom. And you thought taking me to a funeral on our fourth date was strange?"

"Come on," she insisted. "We're stuck here. The only other option is to follow our city's demise on TV."

"Most of it's about sex," I said, hoping to put the kibosh on it. "There was a bit I called, 'The Worst thing About Having Sex with Me.'"

"Sounds fun," said my mom.

Aitana gave me a what-the-hell look. She handed me a comb from her bag. "Here's your microphone, sir."

I got an unexpected rush. Ever since I'd quit I'd been trying to convince myself that performing wasn't for me, and all it took was someone giving me a fake microphone to make me realize how much I loved it: the stage, the people, the late hours, the risk. We do this too much, try to convince ourselves that we don't like something we like, and vice versa, all because of fear.

My mom propped herself up on some pillows. Aitana got giddy as I took "the stage," comb in hand, my back to the long, rectangular window that looked out to the garden where I'd taught myself to juggle a soccer ball.

"So I got to this part after a long chunk about a nasty breakup."

"Yeah, yeah," said Aitana, "just get to it."

"But I know what you all are thinking." Suddenly I was in a club, under the hot lights. "I see it in your faces. You're thinking, *Women actually date this guy?* In fact, some do. Chalk it up or loneliness or lack of options, but why else does anyone date anybody else, anyway? *Women actually have sex with this guy?* They've done that, too, yes. And I can tell what you're thinking now, and you're not mistaken: *That doesn't sound like a pleasant experience for either party involved.*

"YET!" Here I took a too-long pause just like I used to do in my act. "Yet the worst thing about having sex with me is not the actual act of having sex with me. You see, ever since I can remember, I've had a deep fear of fatherhood. I would actually go ahead and say having a son is my worst fear. I'd rather have my arm cut off or be buried alive. What's my second worst fear? Having a daughter."

The daughter tag made Aitana laugh. I looked up. Luz was standing in the doorway holding a tray with our drinks on it, trying to figure out what was going on. I could've told her to come in and leave the tray, but I was in a groove.

"So almost immediately after vaginal penetration, I panic. Because, and I don't know how many of you young people out there know this, but sex is one of the many ways that a woman can end up with a human in her belly. *But Jerónimo, why not just use a condom?* Well, my inquisitive friends, I do use condoms. They're ninety-four to ninety-seven percent effective. Which means that now my brain has to deal with a three to six percent possibility that my worst fear will come true.

"So, ladies, if any of you out there are thinking about having sex with me, and I can sense that some of you might be, just be forewarned that afterwards I'll be contacting you every waking second—we're talking phone calls, texts, Facebook, MySpace, Instagram, Snapchat, Twitter DM, singing telegram, Friendster and messenger pigeon—for every single day until you get your period and I get my freedom back."

It hits me. What I'm doing. Aitana finally looks like she'd rather be somewhere else. Luz has left the tray on the floor and disappeared. My mom has a disquieting expression.

"And it goes on like that," I said.

There is total silence, a comedian's nightmare.

I sit next to Aitana and she holds my hand because she doesn't know what else to do.

My mom turns the volume back up.

HAPHAZARD BIOGRAPHIES OF
MEXICAN PRESIDENTS:
CARLOS SALINAS DE GORTARI
(1988-1994)

We all knew the rumor that he'd killed his maid as a kid, but I thought we all also knew it was nothing more than a rumor. Then, at Mundo's thirtieth birthday party, Eva—who's his ex-girlfriend but was there anyway because they're both so decent and mature—told me that no, it was no rumor, it was the documented truth. "Go ahead," she said, "Google it." I responded that one of my New Year's resolutions was to not use my phone as much, especially in social situations, so we changed the subject. I forgot all about Eva's comment re: the Salinas rumor until a few weeks later, after Martina asked me to meet with her just to let me know that things between us were really over-over. (I suspect she did this because she'd started a new relationship and was feeling pangs of guilt.) Wanting something to distract me, I looked up the rumor, and sure enough, there it was, the front page of the Excélsior dated December 18, 1951: *Playing War, Three Little Children Shoot Maid.* The news story said that, pretending to be soldiers, Gustavo Zapata and Raúl and Carlos Salinas— eight, five, and four years old, respectively—shot and killed their twelve-year-old maid—yes, twelve-year-old maid—Manuela, with a .22-caliber rifle while she was sweeping. When the other maid, María, asked the boys what had happened, they, in turn, screamed with jubilation, "We killed Manuela!" There's a picture of the three kids, and it's easy to recognize Carlos because he already had the same big ears sticking out to the sides as he did when he became president. Toward the end of the story, Carlos is said to be three and not four years old. That's Mexican journalism for you. When asked by the police what had happened, little Carlos said, "I shot her! I'm a hero!" No one was punished for this crime. A couple of years later the Salinas house burned down, and again it was suspected that little Carlos and Raúl were responsible. Carlos went on to major in economics at the National University and earned a Ph.D. from Harvard's Kennedy School of Government with the dissertation *Political Participation, Public Investment, and Support for the System: A Comparative Study of Rural Communities in Mexico*. He became president in 1988 after one of the country's most infamously rigged elections. Salinas negotiated NAFTA and enacted agrarian reform. Remember Raúl, the brother? He was the sort of narco-liaison and head money-launderer during his brother's presidency. In 1995, he was arrested for masterminding the assassination of his former brother-in-law, a crime for which he only served ten years. After his presidency, Carlos fled to Ireland with bags and bags of our money. There was another Salinas brother, by the way, Enrique. He was born a year after the Manuela incident and was murdered in 2004 in his car, suffocated with a plastic bag. I met his daughters during my college days. I had a girlfriend at the time, Perpetua, who was friends with the Salinas girls. I spoke at length with the younger one at a party. I don't remember much, as this was back in 2003, a year before their father's murder. I do remember I found her very attractive in spite of her resemblance to our ex-president, with the classical round face and beady eyes that dominate her family's gene pool. I talked with her about writing because she had dreams of being a screenwriter and I thought I was hot shit for having written and directed a short film. In 2015, both Salinas sisters were outed by the French newspaper *Le Monde* for having hidden assets in a Swiss bank. Asked for comment, they threatened to sue the reporter. The Salinas family didn't even know Manuela's last name. No one ever claimed the dead girl's body.

THE MYSTERIES
OF PATIO VISTAHERMOSA

I

It's been my cross to bear from a very early age (and I understand it's not an uncommon cross) that worrisome thoughts pop into my head as soon as I get in bed at night. As early as seven years old I was robbed of sleep by fears that Katia, whom I thought to be the girl I was destined to marry, hated me. At ten, my qualms turned from the romantic to the mystical-academic: I feared that when I awoke, all my knowledge of multiplication and division would be erased from my brain, and, as a result, I'd be held back a year. Then, in early adolescence, my father lost his job at the ad agency, and, although my mother herself had a good job, I was afraid we'd end up in a homeless shelter where I would inevitably be sexually assaulted. (Over dinner one night, my parents and I had watched a long news piece about the epidemic of sexual crimes in homeless shelters.)

After my father's firing, my problems at school worsened, and then my anxiety reached such levels that it began seeming more like insanity. During my insomniac nights, woven in with ruminations about school, I worried a lot about my father. He was in his short-sleeved blue bathrobe and slippers when I returned from school, when I left for French class at the Alliance Française and when my parents and I sat down at night to eat dinner in front of the television news. He'd stopped playing squash on Saturday mornings and now refused (out of shame—I understood that even then) to attend my mother's family Sunday lunches at my aunt and uncle's. He was a smart and disciplined man: Why had he been fired? What did he do all day? Wasn't he supposed to be looking for another job?

These were only some of the thoughts swirling in my mind during the night when my switch finally flipped. Things inside my head turned violent. I imagined myself torturing and killing my cat. I'd never had a thought like that before. Said cat, Potasio Limantour, named by my father after Norberto de Zúñiga's first minister of Colonization and Industry, was a brown Siamese I loved dearly. Potasio loved me, too—I knew this because every day when I came home from school he climbed up my leg onto my torso. That night, the bad night, however, I couldn't dispel fantasies in which I threw my feline friend against the wall, cut him open from throat to genitals, took his little head and—

It was a horror movie made exclusively for me, and it wouldn't end. The more scared and ashamed I felt about the thoughts, the more violent and vivid they became. I lay in bed for seven hours fighting those horrific scenes, heart pumping and skin tingling, gripping the sheets so I wouldn't run out of my bedroom and murder my cat.

Shortly after the sun came up, as soon as I heard my mother's pumps clack down the stairs and into the kitchen, I went straight to her, squinting so I wouldn't see Potasio.

Alarmed by my droopy, pale face and bloodshot eyes, my mother stopped pouring cereal into a bowl. Potasio slept on one of the island stools.

Back when my father had a job, he'd be the first to wake up every day to make us breakfast. Often, while we enjoyed eggs or French toast, my father would raise his fork like a royal staff and remind us that our kitchen had once been part of Luca Sabaleta's drawing room, the same drawing room where that illustrious man had retreated to for rest and a brandy after assisting in the capture and execution of a dozen rebels during the failed coup of 1903. After the firing, however, I'd rarely see my father before I left for school.

My voice regressed to its prepubescent days when I asked my mother to grab Potasio and keep him away from me.

"You're not feeling well?"

"Mom," back to my regular voice, "grab Potasio."

She did, holding the cat against her chest.

I explained to her that I'd gone crazy and might kill our cat if left unsupervised.

My mother's expression confirmed my suspicion that I was a very dangerous boy. She called to my father who eventually showed up scratching his beard.

"You need to take Luca to a psychiatrist," said my mother. "Now."

And off she went to work.

II

Norberto de Zúñiga ruled this country with an iron fist from 1881 to 1916, when, while delivering one of his infamously long speeches, he was shot, victim to a conspiracy by some of his closest allies. The few members of de Zúñiga's extended cabinet whom the conspirators deemed too loyal to recruit were all killed in some way or another shortly after. Among these loyalists was Luca Sabaleta, de Zúñiga's Undersecretary of the Interior, my great-grandfather and also my namesake.

The history books haven't been kind to Sabaleta, portraying him either as a boneless sycophant or a vicious goon, sometimes both. Yet my father always took great pride in being his grandson.

Sabaleta built himself one of the first mansions in the Patio Vistahermosa neighborhood, which back during the height of de Zúñiga's power wasn't a neighborhood, but a series of rural lands just outside the city. Other de Zuñigistas followed and, before long, the whole place was filled with luxurious homes, all trying to look as European as possible with their mansard roofs, arched windows and balustrades.

By the time I came along, Sabaleta's mansion had been divided and redevided by his descendants. It now comprised eight smallish homes, one of them ours. We were the only Sabaletas who remained living on the property.

III

After a forty-minute chat, the psychiatrist, a bald man in a shirt and tie, told me I had nothing to worry about. Was he joking?

"I almost killed my cat," I said.

He explained that the intrusive thoughts I'd had were nothing more than that—thoughts. I was an anxious boy, he said, and at fourteen my brain was going through some uncomfortable changes. That, added to a difficult situation at home, had led me to an anxiety attack. For many, he concluded nonchalantly, an episode like this is a one-time thing. (This wouldn't be my case, but that's a story for another day.)

I didn't know what to say. This man was telling me that everything that had felt so real an hour ago was nothing. In some ways this calmed me down, and in others it made me feel even crazier.

"What do you enjoy doing the most, Luca?"

"Reading," I blurted. This was not only a lie; it was the biggest of lies. I hated reading, but my father always said that people who didn't read were idiots. Our bookshelves were filled with thick, hardcover history books and bestselling Latin American and European novels. Had I been honest, I would've told the psychiatrist that what I loved doing the most was watching television, preferably shows about detectives chasing criminals.

The doctor responded joyfully to the lie. "Wonderful news," he said. He even added that I looked like a reader, and that, to me, was the best of compliments. "If you're ever feeling a bit anxious, grab a book and lose yourself in it for thirty minutes. That's two birds, one stone: The act of reading will not only help you relax, but it'll be a way to take your psychic temperature. If you can sit down to read, you'll know you're nowhere near an anxiety attack."

IV

During the ride back, driving on Flamboyanes (only a few minutes from home), my father shrieked and pulled over. A flat tire, I thought.

"Look at that!" he said pointing across the street.

A man in an orange vest holding an electric saw was hanging from the branch of a coral tree. There was a small mountain of branches already beneath him.

My father exited the car and raced past the median to the tree, flailing his arms and shouting things I couldn't make out. It appeared he was ordering the man to get down from the coral. This both seemed to amuse and perplex the man in the orange vest, who turned on his noisy electric saw and continued with his activity. There were other workers on the ground and they all shook their head.

Patio Vistahermosa had changed dramatically in the past decade. Many of the mansions had been torn down to make way for buildings; hundred-year-old trees were routinely cut down to accommodate parking entrances; both our local bakery and butcher shop became nightclubs; Parque Libertad, a French-style garden, was replaced by a discount department store.

No one was more heartbroken by this change than my father, for whom the neighborhood was a crucial part of his identity. Ever since I could remember, he'd been lamenting the fall of Patio Vistahermosa, once the crown jewel of the city, an oasis of elegance and class amid the chaos, a reminder of a time when this country still harbored hopes of becoming a world power. My father, when he still had a job, would come home at night, remove his tie, take off his shoes and complain about the valet parking guys who'd colonized Rosas Street, or the fried food stand that had just set up on the corner of Santo Domingo and Izote.

"You don't care?" he'd squeal at my mother for ignoring him. "Ramona, you not only live here, but you're married to the grandson of the de facto founder of this neighborhood!"

"What do you want me to say? Neighborhoods change, cities change, *life* changes." She was a pragmatist. "To fight this is to be eternally frustrated."

And it got worse once my father lost his job. He had too much time and energy on his hands. Leaving the house with him meant hearing endless complaints about the local politician's insatiable greed, or, worse, witnessing a confrontation like the one with the orange-vested men.

The day of my visit to the psychiatrist, my father ended up hailing a police car.

I heard him shout something about permits. The chubby officer attempted to calm him down. "You don't even have a cursory knowledge of the law!" cried my father walking back toward the car. "This city is doomed because of people like you!"

V

The doctor's comment about using reading as a thermometer led me, for the first time, to peruse my home's many bookshelves. Constantly afraid of killing Potasio, now I read every day on the bus ride home (around thirty minutes) to make sure I wasn't close to having an attack; then my cat and I could hug all we wanted. If the bus had been too rowdy for me to concentrate, I'd be very careful not to be left alone with Potasio until I did the required thirty minutes. Sometimes I felt a bit of adrenaline tingling in my stomach or on the back of my legs while watching television and my heart would start pumping faster, harder, so I'd quickly grab the book closest to me and lock myself in my room.

The problem with the thermometer solution was my parents' taste in books. My father's all had titles like *Latin America's Forgotten Modernity* and *The Agrarian Reform: From Latifundia to Neoliberalism*, while my mother's novels told stories of middle-aged couples struggling through marriage.

For weeks, however, I went on like this, reading books I hated, thinking it was a problem with no solution. The book, I thought, was an inherently boring medium created by and for boring people.

Then I met Sócrates López Candil.

VI

I enjoyed spending my afternoons with Potasio watching television, specifically sitcoms on cable, while doing homework. I was addicted to watching American teens wiggle their way out of sticky situations and learn a lesson in the end. (I was certain the cat, too, had come to like the sitcoms—its canned laughter and impossibly bright colors.)

Now, in order to sit and watch television, I had to read fifteen pages or so from one of my parents' dull books. One afternoon, after reading from a brick with a title like *Topography of the Soul*, I grabbed Potasio and turned on the television just to realize that our cable had been shut down. My father's unemployment had hampered his cognitive abilities and it had become common for him to forget to pay the bills. All Potasio and I had for entertainment were the five over-the-air networks.

I flipped from one channel to the next until something—someone—caught my eye on TV Educación, a channel regarded by all as little more than a sedative. The man, who had greasy hair down to his shoulders, sunglasses, and a bright green polyester blazer, sat on a couch looking bored and smoking a cigarette. His name, Sócrates López Candil, was written in digital watch-style font on the bottom of the screen over the word "Writer." The colors and sound quality of the interview, conducted by a woman with puffy hair, placed its original airing somewhere around the late seventies.

This person was a writer? Impossible. He looked less like the authors on the jackets of my mother's books and more like men whom I'd seen stumble out of cantinas.

I couldn't take my eyes off this man: His every move, every word, seemed infinitely interesting. When asked about the upcoming elections, López Candil said we needed a strongman dictator to get rid of all the scum. Prompted with the names of The Great Writers—Reyes, Delibes, Borges (the interviewer pronounced them with reverence)—he responded with either disparaging comments or fake yawns. *What about Octavio Paz?* said the woman with the puffy hair as a last resort. To which López Candil replied he'd first stab himself in the cheek before reading another sentence written by that megalomaniacal sellout. Questioned about his hobbies, my new hero listed old movies, hallucinogenics, billiards, and prostitutes.

As soon as the interview ended, I scanned every bookshelf in my house hoping to find a López Candil. It didn't surprise me to not find a single one. Then I called the local bookstore and got no answer, as they'd closed for the day.

That night at dinner, during a pause in between my father's stories of the destruction of our neighborhood, I mentioned the writer's name. Had they heard of him?

"He's an idiot and a communist," said my father.

My mother was subtler with her disapproval: "If you're interested in literature, I'll gladly lend you a book. I think you'd love Javier Marías."

VII

My school librarian had no idea who I was talking about and recommended, instead, that I check out *The Collected Poems of Rudyard Kipling*.

Later, when the bus dropped me in front of my house, I ran to the used bookstore, scared that my father would worry if I got home too late.

"Do you have anything by Sócrates López Candil?" I said, out of breath, to the gray-haired man who owned the dusty, little shop.

He said nothing and led me to the literature section, where he handed me three raggedy paperbacks: *Little Red Rooster*, *A Coat So Warm*, and *You Are the Desert, but the Desert Is Gone*.

Even though the store was having a clearance sale—that place, too, was being priced out of the neighborhood—I still only had enough money for one book.

"You know," said the gray-haired man, "that's not literature."

It was the best endorsement he could've given López Candil.

I was leafing through the books anxiously, waiting for one to give me a sign—maybe a character named Luca or the description of a naked woman—when the owner, out of pity or impatience, told me I could take all three for the price of one.

I ran back home and hid the three novels in my backpack before opening the door. Of course my father didn't realize I was home twenty-five minutes late. He was lying on the upholstered fainting couch reading the newspaper. I told him I had a stomach ache and would be in my room all afternoon. (Potasio had to stay in the hallway because I hadn't read all day.)

I chose to begin with *You Are the Desert, but the Desert Is Gone* because its cover art was a Hindu goddess holding a rusty sword. The novel was about a couple of college students who, fed up with their respective families (and society in general), decide to elope to the North Desert with plans of eating peyote and getting married by a shaman. The couple spends most of the book wandering around small villages, meeting all sorts of strange characters and experimenting with all kinds of drugs, all the while meditating about life and love. Toward the end of the book, the couple finds the shaman and quickly realizes he's a greedy huckster. Disappointed, they jump on a bus back home and on the way there confess their infidelities to each other.

Before I knew it, it was dark out and I'd read the whole book. I vaguely remembered eating a sandwich at some point in the afternoon and bringing Potasio into the room with me. What a glorious feeling! I was cured!

I slept with the three López Candil books in bed with me and I slept like a baby.

VIII

The following afternoon when I got home from school I wanted to lock myself in my room again, but my father seemed sadder than usual, so I sat in the Louis XV chair close to him.

"Do you remember when I used to take you to the flower market?" he said to me.

Sure I remembered. We went there every Saturday because as a little kid I loved flowers and told people that when I grew up I wanted to be a botanist, a word my father taught me so I'd stop saying I wanted to be a florist.

My father was lying down, staring at the ceiling. Again I asked myself what he did all day. It seemed unconscionable to me that a human being could be home at, say, eleven in the morning.

"They've shut it down," he said. "No more flower market."

"What are they replacing it with?"

My father belted out a cynical laugh. "Who cares?"

I'd spent all day in school secretly reading *Little Red Rooster*, sticking it in thick textbooks during class, taking it with me to a locker room stall during physical education, and retreating to the library during lunch. *Little Red Rooster* turned out to be even better than the book about the desert. The narrator, Matías, was an adolescent from a middle-class family whose parents were getting a divorce due to infidelity. Matías skips school constantly and befriends a gang of bohemians who live in an abandoned mansion that once belonged to a famous actress. The protagonist spends his days with his new friends reading Paul Valéry, drinking whiskey, smoking pot, taking mushrooms, listening to the blues on vinyl, and stealing food from grocery stores. When the bus driver shouted at me that it was my stop—I'd been so immersed in the story that I lost track of time and space—Matías was huffing paint thinner in an empty swimming pool with a pretty bohemian girl, possibly about to lose his virginity.

So I just said some platitudes about the flower market to my father and ran up to my room, feeling more than a little guilty, eager to finish the book.

I was relieved to read that Matías did in fact lose his virginity in that empty swimming pool with the pretty bohemian (who turned out to be the famous actress's niece). I read the scene maybe ten times and then masturbated as Potasio eyed me from the corner of the room.

IX

When the bus dropped me off at school the next morning, I retreated to the little wooded area behind the faculty parking lot where no one could see me. Once the bell rang and everyone shuffled into buildings and classrooms, I jumped the fence out to the street.

Although I attended a private school, it was located in a dangerous part of the city. As soon as my feet hit the hard pavement of the curb, I, for the first time, yearned for the safety of my classes, for its predictability and familiarity.

When a couple of shady guys across the street who'd seen what I'd done chuckled, I noticed one of them barely had any teeth.

I could've easily gone back to school—jumped the fence again or told the security guard at the entrance that I'd missed the bus and my father had dropped me off—but what would López Candil think of me then? The people who did stuff like that in his novels were fools.

In my backpack was a Discman loaded with the only blues CD I'd found in my house (my parents listened mostly to classical music) titled *Eric Clapton Does the Blues*. Sadly, from the cover I could tell that this Clapton fellow was white, and Matías's bohemians said that blues was a genre of music that could only be interpreted properly by African-Americans because of their heritage of slavery. My plan was to walk around listening to the CD until I found something cool like an abandoned mansion, a group of bohemians or a pretty girl, but I was scared to take out the Discman for fear I'd get mugged. I'd never really looked at my school's surroundings until now, at its graffittied walls and empty lots with broken windows.

A strange hand on my shoulder made me yelp. It belonged to a tall homeless man with a long, white beard who mumbled something about cancer. I said "No thanks" and walked away as the guys who'd chuckled at me before now started to cackle.

I walked faster and faster in the direction of Avenida Colmenar, where at least there was traffic and I could scream if someone tried to rob me. The street vendors called out offering fried foods, pornographic VHS tapes, and other things I'd been taught were harmful for the body and soul. I was scared for my Discman, a Christmas present from an aunt, but I was even more scared that my parents' Eric Clapton CD would get stolen. How would I explain this to them? Was that marijuana I smelled?

When I finally arrived at the corner of Colmenar, winded, I found a decent diner filled with people in cheap office wear, and my heartbeat retreated somewhere close to its normal rate.

I sat at one of the booths next to the window and ordered a coffee. I'd never had coffee before, but the characters in López Candil's novels loved drinking it when hungover and waxing philosophical. I wiped the sweat off my face with a paper napkin before taking *A Coat So Warm* from my bag, feeling a tingle in my stomach as I turned to the first page.

During the following weekends, I'd make several trips to the National Library to do research on López Candil. There, I learned that *A Coat So Warm* was the writer's failed attempt at Serious Literature, a book that he thought would put him amongst the writers he claimed to loathe. Longer than his previous two novels put together and written in a baroque stream-of-consciousness style, the book was panned and even mocked by the critics, sending López Candil into a deep depression and back to the industrial town where he was born. He taught literature there at a public school until his death of liver failure at the age of forty-one. That day at the diner, however, I was sure that I couldn't get past page six of *A Coat So Warm* because of a failure on my part—I was dumb and López Candil was a genius.

Without anything else to read, I turned to Clapton's whiny guitar and raspy voice:

Have you ever loved a woman so much you tremble in pain?

All the time you know she bears another man's name.

After about an hour and two coffee refills, the manager informed me that if I wasn't planning on ordering any food, I'd have to leave. This wouldn't happen now, but back then kids in this city were still second-class citizens.

My plan was to return to Patio Vistahermosa and hang out there until the time that the school bus usually dropped me off at my house. Without money for a taxi (or even the knowledge of how much a taxi would cost), I decided to walk up smoggy Colmenar to where I could hop on a trolley that would take me straight to what had once been Parque Libertad.

The walk was longer than I'd calculated and Colmenar smelled of gasoline, garbage and shit, so by the time I got on the trolley I was sweaty and cranky. I sat at the back and ate the lunch my mother had made for me—a sandwich and two bananas—while chiding myself for not befriending a group of bohemians.

It was almost noon when the trolley dropped me off. With three hours to spare, I first went into a CD shop and scrutinized the blues section, making a mental list of which CDs I'd buy once I got my birthday money. I leafed through the gossip magazines at a newsstand in search of bikini-clad celebrities until the newsstand guy told me to buy something or leave. I even went to a furniture store to waste time, sitting on the couches and chairs, ranking them on comfort level.

Then I saw my father while walking down Flamboyanes.

At first I didn't think it could be him, because this man, who looked so much like my father, had actual clothes on: khakis, a tucked-in plaid shirt, and a black baseball cap. He was sitting at a sidewalk table of the legendary Café Nápoles having an espresso and reading the newspaper and it was definitely him.

The first thought I had was that he was waiting for his mistress. (It was a theory heavily influenced by López Candil's novels, which all, in some way or another, dealt with infidelity.) Everything made sense now. My father had been fired from his job because he'd been having an affair with his boss's wife. The tryst had ruined my father, but still, he couldn't stop seeing her.

I sat on the bench of the ample median that was somewhat hidden by shrubbery. I wanted to see the woman who'd destroyed my family. Would she be much younger than my mother? Would she be beautiful? Should I confront them? How would this play out if I was a character created by López Candil?

Eventually, however, my father finished his espresso, paid for it and left. But the mystery continued, as he wasn't walking in the direction of our house, but toward Avenida Central. I followed him from afar, feeling the adrenaline in my arms and chest.

We walked past what was once Mr. Fernando's liquor store, now a 7-Eleven, and what used to be the Egyptian restaurant, now a bank.

I followed him for about ten minutes until we reached the flower market. My father walked over to its chain-link fence as I stayed in the corner, half my body hidden by a new building.

My father tried to open the gate, but it was locked. What used to be a whole block of bright colors and pungent smells was now nothing but hot concrete.

Again my father tried to pull the gate open. Was he remembering the both of us walking down those aisles hand in hand? Imagining scenes of what he'd once hoped his life would be? Was he having a deep conversation with Luca Sabaleta?

My instinct was to run up and hug him, but of course I couldn't.

A PAINLESS ETHICS

PRE-SHOW, 5:30-6:59 A.M.

Benjamín felt something off on the set of *¡Mañanitas!*
But things there were always off. Exempli gratia: One
morning, Saraí—an impossibly curvy young woman who
co-anchored the show in skimpy outfits—was caught
naked in her dressing room with her (also naked) nutri-
tionist by her paranoid (turns out, with good reason) husband, a gym rat congressman. All three parties were either
on cocaine or pills or both. Screaming ensued. The congressman had to be restrained by three security guards
and a gaffer.

Drugs played a big part in why things went awry on
the set of *¡Mañanitas!* The talent had a penchant for late-
night parties and their call time, Monday through Friday,
was 6 a.m., so they all used something to level them out.
Sometimes it did more than that. One example was when
Carruco Garza Prado, a former telenovela heartthrob
turned *¡Mañanitas!* co-anchor who dressed in three-piece
tweed suits, ran through a thick-glass door and had to be
rushed to the emergency room. His beautiful face would
never be the same, and so the network let him go before
he was even released from the hospital.

No, no. Most days something was off, but this morning it was off-off. (Things that are always off can still be off in comparison to their normal offness.) Benjamín could feel it thick in the air. And there was evidence to back it up, too. Producers whispering to each other, huddled in corners; Mimi Pelayo, the face of *¡Mañanitas!*, wiping away a makeup-covered tear; people talking on one phone and furiously texting on another; and so on.

Of course, nobody informed Benjamín of anything. The higher-ups looked down on him as a measly set PA, while his fellow lower-downs didn't trust him due to his pale skin, rich-kid way of talking, and the fact that he sat alone to read during breaks.

Still, even though something was off-off, everyone went through their usual routine. This included Benjamín. The set of *¡Mañanitas!* was enormous and decorated as the audience of the show (women, class B-- and lower, according to OSH&W's audience catalogue) thought a wealthy person's home looked like: big sofas with colorful pillows, floor lamps, chandeliers, silk flowers in baroque vases, a spiral staircase that went nowhere, et alii. Benjamín's job was to assist in carrying any furniture that needed to be moved (and furniture constantly needed to be moved) as well as to keep everything looking shiny.

INTRO, 7:00-7:05 A.M.

¡Mañanitas! first aired in 1999 as a two-hour telenovela recap/celebrity gossip show. Fifteen years later,

as the once-mighty networks writhed in the age of new media, *¡Mañanitas!*, now airing from 7 a.m. to noon and turned into an all-encompassing morning show, remained a cash cow.

They got the lead in from Pedro Vallelazcano, the perfectly coiffed, son-of-an-actual-print-journalist host of the morning news. Vallelazcano ended his hour with pieces from the entertainment world. Then a split screen showed him on the (audience's) left and Mimi's (always) ecstatic face on the right. They bantered about one of the puff pieces and then flirted a bit. (The B-- and lowers couldn't get enough of this will-they-won't-they even though—especially because—both were married.) Sometimes they even traded some safe yet off-color innuendo.

Today the puff piece was that Will Smith (Will Smith!) would be sitting for a one-on-one with Vallelazcano the following week as part of the actor's Latin American tour to promote his newest movie.

It unsettled Benjamín how little Mimi praised Vallelazcano re: this get of gets. In the world of *¡Mañanitas!* Will Smith was as big and unattainable as Jesus Christ or Deepak Chopra. Mimi Pelayo (#1 fan of both Jesus Christ and Deepak Chopra) had interviewed three presidents, but never a Hollywood star of the stature of Smith. She tried her best, but just couldn't muster up the enthusiasm.

Benjamín, crouching next to a Louis XV chair, panicked. There could only be one reason for things to be this much off. *¡Mañanitas!* would be getting canceled. Which meant that he'd be out of a job. And the baby? Lucrecio. (He had to remember to call the baby by his name.)

Time to move the Louis XV to Zone IV! The TVs of the B-- and lowers were now full-screen *¡Mañanitas!* The seven co-anchors stood side by side in Zone I dancing to a popular '80s or '90s song. Today it was El Símbolo's "Uno, dos, tres," the audio director's fave. The camera panned from (audience's) left to right as each host danced in a self-conscious/wacky/sexy way looking, straight at the camera. There were Carlos Trigo, mid-forties, Garza Prado's replacement, who also dressed as a 1950's intel-lectual; Sofiana, early thirties, former beauty queen who always dressed in black or red evening gowns; Hugo Ernesto, an Argentinian silver fox who donned creased jeans and an untucked shirt; Saraí; Mimi Pelayo, the only remaining member of the original cast, who day after day wore the same style of miniskirt she did back in 1999; El Perro, a twenty-something prankster; and, finally, Panuchito the Clown, a clown, age unknown, everything unknown.

A new energy rose inside Benjamín as he dragged two sequined beanbag chairs to Zone III. It was stupid to think the network would cancel the show. It was all they had. That and soccer. And even soccer was showing its lowest numbers in years. There was no way *¡Mañanitas!* would be cancelled. Which meant something else was wrong. The energy went away. That possibility was even scarier.

WE MUST TALK ABOUT THIS BABY, LUCRECIO, PART 1 OF 5

The day after he met Bárbara Sabatini at the wrap party for the National Company for the Dramatic Arts' (CNAD, for its acronym in Spanish) run of *The Seagull*, Benjamín spoke of her to Emanuel, his only real friend, as a man in love. Which he never did. Most of the time he spoke as a jaded man and sometimes as a man foreseeing the apocalypse. (He'd been hopeful about his acting career back then, but wouldn't have dared admit it to anyone.) Emanuel was all raised eyebrows. "Seems like a catch."

Benjamín had originally planned to act in *The Seagull*. His favorite character was, of course, Boris, though he knew he was too young for the part, so he'd settle for Konstantin. Besides, he'd seen Alicio Jardiner play Konstantin and it was a borderline life-changing experience. Alicio Jardiner, who once had said that he'd play a tree in order to be on stage.

While preparing his thesis monologue at the Royal British Northern Conservatory & Academy of the Performing Arts, Durham—from Pinter's *The Caretaker*—he kept an eye out online for the CNAD's casting call for *The Seagull* and practiced a few key Konstantin scenes. (He'd found out they'd be staging the Chekhov play because he'd read an interview with Rogelio D.M., famous CNAD director, in which he'd mentioned it.) One day he rehearsed his thesis and the next his audition.

The casting calls never came.

Hours after returning from England, Benjamín took a taxi to the CNAD. It was an enormous campus in the southern part of the city that contained a school, several theaters and a popular art house cinema. The grassy areas were populated by stoned youths, actors rehearsing their lines, and students doing homework or reading.

Rogelio D.M.'s office was in the top floor of a five-story building way at the back of the campus. "I'd like to speak to Rogelio," said Benjamín to the receptionist, as if his UK MA gave him the right to waltz into any director's or producer's office and demand a role. She told him he wasn't in. "I'll wait," he said.

"Some days he doesn't come at all," she said.

Benjamín waited. Almost two hours. He'd brought a book. Rogelio D.M. showed up wearing a green suit, a purple paisley shirt and a purple paisley tie, sunglasses, beret, and lit cigarillo.

In his office, Rogelio D.M. told Benjamín he didn't take meetings, and he didn't seem at all impressed by the RBNC&APA. *The Seagull* was already in rehearsals, cast by actors that belonged to the CNAD. "But I will do you a favor," said Rogelio. "You can work in the production of *The Seagull* as a stagehand. In a trainee capacity. Or intern. Whatever they're calling it these days. I would even pay you, but the union would chop my head off. It's a great opportunity for someone like you. Get your feet wet. An actor must be a man of the theater. He must be a writer, director, stagehand, lighting designer."

The baby, Lucrecio, hasn't been mentioned yet, but we're getting there.

NIVEA YOGA CORNER, 7:49-7:53 A.M.

The show's producers loved, loved, loved the fact that besides being handsome and appearing to have zero percent body fat, Juan Zhang was of Chinese descent. In the meeting re: the possibility of hiring Zhang as the *¡Mañanitas!* yoga instructor, in which Benjamín handled the coffee and waters, someone mentioned that wasn't yoga originated in India or Japan and not China? This caused laughter. If they weren't sure where yoga originated, the B-- and lowers surely would have no idea. A network (marketing?) suit who hadn't said a word so far and instead had been interacting with his tablet, informed the room that one of the unexpected results they'd had in a couple of *¡Mañanitas!* focus groups was the audience's deep prejudice against Asians. A producer projected on the whiteboard a full-body photograph of Juan in black tights and nothing else. "Look at him," she said. "He's fucking gorgeous. And he doesn't even look that Chinese, just enough to give the segment credibility." Credibility was also why the Nivea Yoga Corner graphic was musicalized with Charles Douglas's "Kung-Fu Fighting."

Mispronouncing Zhang's name was a running gag for the *¡Mañanitas!* co-hosts, but this morning Saraí—now in tiny shorts and a sports bra nailing the cow pose—was overdoing it. She was desperate, had already gone through Sing, Ping, Ching, Tong, and Ming. Benjamín knew it had to be a symptom of her trying to hide whatever was worrying them.

"Now this next pose," said Zhang in a full lotus, "is only for my advanced students, like the beautiful Saraí. It's called the half side plank."

Benjamín almost fainted when he saw Pepe Gandoya talking to a producer. Right there, on the floor. Pepe Gandoya! A few feet from Benjamín. This could only mean the end times.

WE MUST TALK ABOUT THIS BABY, LUCRECIO, PART 2 OF 5

The Seagull's run was a complete success (as much as a play can be a success in a country where people have absolutely no interest in anything related to the theater.) But it was painful for Benjamín to watch the CNAD's (in his opinion) third-rate actors butcher one of his favorite plays night after night—the melodramatic deliveries, the flimsy stage presence, the constant shouting! He did a lot of drinking during those months. He was also, however, confident that he'd be a shoo-in for company membership. If those idiots could do it, he surely could as well. Besides, he'd had a few short but deep conversations with Rogelio D.M. re: Pinter and Albee. Networking!

As it's been established, Benjamín was not great at making friends. (Or if it hasn't been explicitly established, then it's been implied.) Although working in the production of a play often makes close friends of complete strangers, Benjamín ended the run without having established a single new relationship. But he had to go to the wrap party anyway. So he decided he'd be there for half an hour and leave.

The house was old, immense, and cluttered with Persian rugs, Greek replica sculptures, framed production posters, metal plaques commemorating productions, and books—books everywhere. Rogelio D.M.'s wife, dressed in a pink kimono, was the life of the party. By the time Benjamín got there, most everybody was drunk and/or stoned.

There was a woman that caught his eye. (Yes, it was Bárbara Sabatini, who was there because she knew several of the actors.) Her hair was cut short and parted to the side, typical of women who are confident in their beauty. But her face wasn't so much beautiful as it was interesting. Which was exactly what attracted Benjamín to her. She had popping eyes, a long nose and a small mouth. She caught him a couple of times staring at her, at that interesting face, at her fashionable outfit of a beige cashmere sweater, tight black jeans, and patent leather shoes with no socks.

Benjamín had never been able to approach attractive women. Often he just looked at them until they realized he was looking at them and it made him feel like a creep. He felt like a creep at Rogelio D.M.'s party and decided to leave—without saying good-bye to anyone, as was his wont.

Walking to his car he heard someone calling him. It was her. "Where are you going?"

He almost apologized. "Um. Home."

"Where do you live?" He told her.

"Good. I live around there, too. Give me a ride."

She suggested they stop at a bar along the way for one more drink and lit a joint on the ride over. (Benjamín had quit weed because twenty-eight percent of the time it gave him panic attacks.) He took her to a German beer bar he liked because it made him feel like he was in Munich. Benjamín had never been to Munich. Bárbara mentioned she'd done a semester abroad in Berlin. "You have to go to Berlin." She did her master's at the Université Paris-Sud. Ph.D. from the prestigious Universidad Musonia de Ciencias y Artes. Now she taught at that same institution. Twentieth-century philosophy. Her specialty were the post-structuralists.

Benjamín was impressed by all of this. (He'd read Deleuze and Guattari in college and almost vomited in confusion.) He sold himself to her as a shoo-in for the CNAD and exaggerated his relationship with Rogelio D.M.

Later they went to his apartment and got naked. Her body was a contradiction. Petite yet boxy. Elegant. Small breasts. He thought of her as a 1980s Volvo. (What would French post-structuralism think of that? Actually, he had no idea.) She was perfect.

PHILOSOPHY FOR YOU, PRESENTED BY BANCO FAMILIA, 9:09-9:18 A.M.

During the past few years, Mimi Pelayo had gotten progressively more into mysticism, holism, and esotericism.

Also, anything inspirational. During one of the rare times in which Vallelazcano's throw-to banter took on a solemn tone—the day Mimi's daughter graduated from secondary school—Mimi told the news anchor that as she aged she was beginning to think of herself more as a philosopher than an entertainer. She was finally realizing the responsibility she carried by anchoring (she'd said "anchoring" and not "co-anchoring," which caused the biggest of dramas) one of the highest-rated shows in this great country's history of television.

The *¡Mañanitas!* staff wasn't blindsided by this. She constantly talked about the Kabbalah and the book of poems she was working on. Every day she read the Tarot cards to different members of the makeup and wardrobe crew. She was always carrying books by Paulo Coelho and Miguel Ruiz. She wore beads and bracelets with obscure and not-so-obscure meanings. One day, during a backstage shouting match with El Perro, she predicted he'd never achieve Pure Happiness or get to know the Real God or much less understand the Truth.

She lobbied for a new section about important topics—something more than just entertainment. The production respected Mimi Pelayo's looks and charisma, but not her foresight. They gave her the go-around, saying they were focus-grouping it and talking it up to the always-reticent suits. When she'd had enough of the lying, Mimi Pelayo stopped showing up. Three days were enough for the network to cave. They offered her a two-minute-and-forty-second segment three times a week where she could address serious things.

Now, a bit over a year later, *Philosophy for You*, co-anchored by Mimi, Carlos, and Sofiana, was a nine-minute daily segment in which the three interviewed priests, self-help gurus, life coaches, neo-shamans, business leaders, Buddhists, couples therapists, Olmec spiritualists, et alii. It was second in ratings only to the cooking segment. *Philosophy for You* even had its own Instagram account, with hundreds of thousands of followers, where Mimi Pelayo's assistant posted the best quotes from each day's segment with a picture of a waterfall or a forest or a Buddha as the backdrop.

Today, of course, the segment, like the rest of the show, was falling flat as a pancake. Mimi, Carlos, and Sofiana were asking half-assed questions to an angelologist, while the set's attention was on Pepe Gandoya, PR enforcer and right-hand man to the network's vice president, who was now talking with a very serious face (the only one he had) to Vallelazcano's protégé, Paulina Altimbar, who anchored the news segment. Smoking was prohibited in the studios, but not for Gandoya. He was puffing on an enormous cigar.

Even Mimi Pelayo kept looking over at Gandoya.

Benjamín, who'd been given the task of wiping a four-foot ersatz-metal spoon with a moist towel, could see the fear on everyone's faces. OK, the show wouldn't get canceled, but something horrible had or was about to happen. Benjamín saw the distorted reflection of his own terrified face on the spoon. Money! Up until recently it was something he never thought about, even derided people who chased it. Now it clouded his days and kept him up at nights. Money. Because of the baby. Lucrecio. The guilt led to hopelessness.

"It's very important to put a glass of sugared water next to the flowers," said the angelologist. "Clean water, not tap water. Then open all the windows at sundown."

The only person completely oblivious to Gandoya was Sofiana's daughter, Marilyn Denisse. She was around ten. Very much overweight. Benjamín noticed her sitting on a black cube, playing with a tablet, wearing a beanie with the stitched face of a monkey on the front. Sofiana took her to work whenever the girl for whatever reason didn't go to school. Benjamín guessed schools had been canceled that day due to the windstorm. "She loves the whole showbiz lifestyle," Sofiana always told everyone. In truth, Benjamín liked Marylin Denisse because she seemed to be the only person who hated *¡Mañanitas!* than he did. He'd tried to talk to her several times, but the child was much too shy.

He carried the spoon over to the girl, hoping that this bit of whimsy might get her to open up.

"Hey," he said. "Watcha playin'?"

"A game," she responded without looking up.

"Oh. I'm holding a giant spoon."

"Uh huh."

WE MUST TALK ABOUT THIS BABY, LUCRECIO, PART 3 OF 5

Bárbara told Benjamín she was pregnant three weeks after breaking up with him. They talked and talked trying to figure something out. Also talked about their lives, their families, other people's lives, and so on. He confessed to her for the first time that he hadn't gotten selected for the CNAD.

"But you were a shoo-in," she said in a voice he found mocking. "You told me that the night we met."

"I thought it was the truth."

"Nobody had actually told you you were a shoo-in."

"How could they if the auditions hadn't happened yet?"

Now she looked at him with pity. "You really actually don't know how the world works, do you? I thought that was only half true and half self-parody."

"What are you talking about?"

She explained to him that everyone in the art and academia scenes knew that auditions had nothing to do with CNAD membership. The three-page creative statement was even more irrelevant. And no one even looked at the CV.

The CNAD had a board with X number of members. "You do at least know that, right?"

"Of course." (He didn't.)

The number of new actors depended on how many of the current actors' contracts run out and how much money the federal government has allocated for the CNAD on any given year. Once the number of new members (y) was defined, they divided it by the number of board members. Each board member then got the right to pick z number of incoming actors—usually their friends, friends' relatives, students, lovers, et cetera. She drew the equation on his forearm with a black Sharpie:

$x/y=z$

"Do you see yourself anywhere in that equation?"

The whole application process was just a formality for the CNAD to pretend that its taxpayer-funded process was honest and open. By the time Benjamín had gone to his audition—and how he'd prepared!—the new actors had already been picked.

"You could've told me this sooner."

"I was sure an x had you as a z."

A lot of confessions were made during the lockdown. More confessions the more tired they got. Until finally she confessed that she'd already decided what they were going to do.

OH, GOD: A PARENTHETICAL

Bárbara was part of a new intellectual group that called itself neo-traditionalism. All Benjamín knew about it was that they met weekly and were preparing a book of essays to present themselves to the world. He was so tired and scared and hungry that he could barely understand her now as she tried to tell him the details of this movement to him for the first time. There was a lot about "re-respecting the family nucleus." She said the phrase "freedom of constrainment." He told her it sounded like the opposite of post-structuralism. She mentioned Lipovetsky, Benbraham, and the rejection of a painless ethics.

WE MUST TALK ABOUT THIS BABY, LUCRECIO, PART 3 OF 5 (CONT'D)

According to Bárbara, as part of this movement, it would be hypocritical of her (and damaging to the neo-traditionalists as a whole) to have an abortion.

"No one would find out," he said.

"How are you so innocent?"

Then he listed the only things he knew to be true:

1. He wasn't ready to be a father.

2. He didn't have any money.

3. He was unemployed.

4. Due to his own sad childhood, he feared that having a child of his own would bring to the forefront terrible trauma he'd worked hard to suppress.

"Like I said, Benja, the decision has been made. By me. The person in which the baby is going to grow."

"So this child will have unwed parents? A weekend father? Does that jibe with neo-traditionalist ideas?"

TELENOVELAS RECAP, PRESENTED BY SUPERTIENDAS CARMONA, 9:51-10:17

Pepe Gandoya had left. Now on set was Mikel, the *¡Mañanitas!* director, who had facial paralysis on his right side due to a stroke. Mikel had been fired several times from the network because his addiction problems stood out even among all of the network's employees' addiction problems. (After one of the firings he spent years living in a flophouse smoking crack.)

But the suits liked Mikel. As long as he was kept out of trouble, he got things done. In fact, he was so efficient that he hardly directed at all. Most of his time was spent up in the control booth chewing on nicotine gum and his fingernails. And it worked!

The co-anchors of the telenovelas recap—Mimi, Saraí, Hugo Ernesto, and Panuchito—sat in perpendicular couches (pistachio green and pink, Zone V) getting their makeup retouched during the commercial break as Benjamín and another stagehand quickly installed the flat screen. Mikel paced in front of the couches, pensive.

"It's all taken care of," he said through the left side of his mouth. "The execs freaked out at the beginning, but those motherfuckers always freak out!"

The cast tried to laugh at this.

Benjamín loved to do his Mikel impression to Bárbara and Emanuel. It was mean, but it always made them laugh. Mikel had directed so many telenovelas that he'd completely forgotten how human beings actually behaved.

"I just had a smoke outside with Gandoya. Is he mad? Fucking furious! But I've known that son of a bitch for over thirty years. They pay him those millions because he *fixes shit*. Got it?"

The co-anchors nodded.

"I've been watching the show from up on the booth and cannot believe my eyes. You've been doing this whole show with your heads up your asses. Because of this silly, gossip bullshit? You're *pro-fe-ssion-als*." Mikel pointed his finger at each of the anchors. "That means the show must go on! You know who said that? Freddy

Mercury! One of the greatest artistic minds in the history of this glorious blue marble!"

The others mumbled apologies.

"Don't apologize!" said Mikel. "Fix it. Millions of people start their day with this show. It's what gives them energy, hope. It's their goddamn morning prayer! You. Are. Important. To. Them. They. Count. On. You."

WE MUST TALK ABOUT THIS BABY, LUCRECIO, PART 4 OF 5

The more she spoke, the clearer it became to Benjamín that Bárbara was using their situation not to merely abide by the neo-traditionalist model of a family, but to create it. They'd get married, for the child, and raise it together. Mother and father. Like in the old days. (Neither Bárbara nor Benjamín had grown up in a two-parent household.) But each would have the liberty to explore their own sexual/sentimental extramarital relationships.

Bábara came from a wealthy family—a long line of politicians on her mother's side and a hotelier father. She owned a nice two-bedroom where they could live rent-free. They would share a room, but sleep in separate twin beds with a nightstand between them.

Why did Benjamín agree to this nonsense? Again, a list. (Sorry.)

1. His impending fatherhood had made money The Biggest of Deals, and this way he wouldn't have to pay rent.
2. Benjamín was the son of an absentee father and thus not ignorant of how much growing up sans male role model could eff up one's psyche.
3. It was clear to him that Bárbara was destined to be successful. Famous, even. A big deal, maybe. Which meant that neo-traditionalism would be big as well. And he hated thinking it, but the cachet of being part of neo-traditionalism's First Family appealed to him. Would he be mocked as Bárbara's tool, her plaything? Sure. Would it give a much-needed boost to his acting career? (And he hated thinking this way.) Most definitely.
4. He loved Bárbara. She was a bit of a narcissist, aloof toward those she didn't deem worthy of her (which were most), and seemed to feel absolutely nothing for Benjamín anymore, but he couldn't help himself. Other things she was were brilliant, gorgeous, stylish, and ambitious.

Benjamín called *The Seagull*'s stage manager about working a paying job at another production. His former boss told him he could probably get him work as a stagehand in television. Which is how he ended up in *¡Mañanitas!*

As soon as he set foot on the set that first morning, he couldn't help but think of Alicio Jardiner.

MICE AND/OR MEN

During his preparatory school days, Benjamín spent most of his time at the Teatros Campo, a cluster of state-subsidized theaters where one could watch somewhat decent shows. Many days he'd drive there directly from school, eat a sandwich at the rundown cafeteria, and buy a ticket for whichever play was on next. After that he often bought a ticket for an evening play. He saw every production several times.

Alicio Jardiner was always in a Teatros Campo play. And he was always the best actor on stage. The theatre community all agreed that he was the next great actor. Watching him pushed Benjamín from thinking he might give acting a shot, to knowing that the only thing he ever wanted to be was an actor. When he learned that Jardiner had an MA from a British university, he decided he'd get one himself when the time came. He'd be the next Alicio Jardiner.

Then, when Benjamín went on to university and began attending hipper, more underground venues, something happened to the star actor. Mental health stuff, mainly. Which led to the abuse of pills. He went from doing plays to acting in telenovelas for the same network that aired *¡Mañanitas!* (Jardiner visited the show several times.) The man turned into a punch line—a lazy sellout who sold his talent for easy money.

There was a lot of anger directed at Jardiner, and with it came many rumors. He'd been Mimi Pelayo's lover; one of the suits' boy toy; made a fortune dealing synthetic drugs to all the television pseudo-actors; pimped underage prostitutes to lusty cameramen. Impossible to know which were true and which weren't, but the ballad of Alicio Jardiner became a dark one.

He got fired after a violent incident. Disappeared from the face of the Earth. A new set of rumors popped up, and the most trustworthy ones spoke of him working children's parties.

All of this, of course, was a terrible blow to Benjamín.

THE NEWS, 10:32-10:37 A.M.

Today it was Mimi Pelayo's turn to co-anchor the news segment with Paulina Altimbar, but the *¡Mañanitas!* staple had stormed off the set. Mikel scrambled, trying to get Saraí to be in the segment, but she was furious with Mimi. Finaly, it was Hugo Ernesto who sat down with Paulina to chat about current events.

WE MUST TALK ABOUT THIS BABY, LUCRECIO, PART 5 OF 5

The pregnancy was a breeze. Bárbara followed a strict diet rich in calcium and vitamin D. She frequented yoga class, did low-impact aerobics, and took breaks from gravity in her father's swimming pool. Her papers were being published in prestigious academic journals. The same-room-separate-beds situation took some getting used to, but eventually Benjamín settled into it. At night, they talked with the lights off until one of them dozed off. It was as if they were siblings.

Then, tragedy. The baby was born with a rare heart condition that had him in a sort of coma. Bárbara visited him Mondays, Wednesdays, and Fridays, while Benjamín went to the hospital on Tuesdays, Thursdays, and Saturdays. They went together on Sundays.

Benjamín often skipped his visiting days because it was too much for him to go and watch this baby, Lucrecio, all alone, confused, helpless in a translucent box. They wouldn't even let him hold him. All he could do was look from afar next to other worried parents.

The neo-traditionalist patient zero couple barely talked anymore. They were too tense. The baby, Lucrecio, if he came out of this alive, would have health issues for the rest of his life, but now they were clinging to the hope that his brain would come out intact. The longer he stayed in that sort of coma the lower the chances were of that happening.

Benjamín didn't even want to name the baby until he was released from the hospital. Bárbara said that was stupid and coldhearted and named him Lucrecio Gilberto, after the Roman philosopher and her politician grandfather. He said it was a pretentious name and often referred to the baby as "the baby." This infuriated her. He was the father and would call Lucrecio by his name, like a normal person.

OUTRO & POST-SHOW

The show ended as it began. The co-anchors lined up shoulder to shoulder, dancing. Mimi Pelayo wasn't there, of course. The other co-anchors seemed dismayed—except for Panuchito the Clown, who seemed to be more stoned than usual. (He was euphoric and had thick, transparent snot sliding down his left nostril.) Benjamín wondered if the B-- and lowers had noticed how strange the show had been that day.

After cleaning up with the rest of the crew, he approached his boss and asked what had been going on all day. The guy told him not to worry. Benjamín knew that what that really meant was, You're not one of us.

THERE ARE PEOPLE WHO KNOW THINGS AND PEOPLE WHO DON'T

Instead of driving straight home, he stopped at his favorite diner. Whereas before the baby, Lucrecio, he'd eat there all the time, now he did it only sparingly and couldn't fully enjoy it because of the guilt it caused him to spend money. Eating out made questions pop into his head, questions like, would he ever make a decent living? Was it irresponsible of him to continue to pursue acting now that he had a son? He ordered scrambled eggs and ate while reading from his *Pocket Anthology of German Expressionist Drama (1917-32)*.

The wind storm came in bursts. It had woken him up the night before, and now the windows of the diner began to rattle. He'd never been in a windstorm before, hadn't even really known that there was such a thing, and decided it was the stupidest of the natural disasters and semi-disasters. A blizzard at least had beauty to it, and tornados were cinematic. Windstorms were invisible and just made everybody anxious. Hundreds of trees and a dozen billboards had fallen over. Stupid.

At home, Bárbara was lying on the couch with her MacBook on her lap. Benjamín took the other couch. Usually he changed immediately because it embarrassed him to wear his one-piece uniform in front of her. (Bárbara was wearing polka-dot leggings, a light denim shirt with the sleeves rolled up, and an enormous gold watch.) Today he just didn't have the energy to care.

"Don't forget it's your turn to visit Lucrecio."

"Something's wrong with the show," said Benjamín, eyes closed.

"Yeah, no shit," she said as she typed.

Benjamín's eyes opened. He sat up. "You watched it?"

"Did I watch ¡*Mañanitas!*? No, dear. Fortunately, I have better things to do." She closed her laptop and placed it on the coffee table. "But it's all over social media. I texted you about it."

His phone. Benjamín tapped his pockets. He'd forgotten to take it with him. The only thing people seemed to admire about him was his detachment from his phone, but it only seemed to hurt him.

"What happened?"

"You seriously don't know? You spent all morning there."

"But no one speaks to me! I carry furniture around and clean a giant spoon."

"Something happened to …."

"To whom?"

Bárbara forced a sigh. "Jardiner."

As if melting, Benjamín laid back on the couch. His quilt. Where was his quilt? He wanted to wrap himself up in it forever. "Where's my damn quilt?"

"I know he meant a lot to you."

He mustered up all his strength to sit upright. "Meant?"

Instantly he knew it had been a suicide.

"Remember the rumors about him working children's parties?"

"They were true?"

She nodded. "They found him dressed in a minion mascot suit."

"A what?"

"Don't be a snob, Benja. You're perfectly aware of minions."

She knew him well. Minions were those yellow anthropomorphic pills from a kids' movie that adults (who in the times of post-late-capitalism were rewarded for having the intellectual standards of an eight-year-old) also watched. He'd seen those things in billboards everywhere. Hated them with a passion.

"The poor thing went mad. His husband found him in the bathtub."

"Dressed like a fucking *minion*?"

"He'd slit his wrists."

Wire-rim glasses off. Hands on face. Tears. Was this the beginning of one of his panic attacks?

"Again, I'm sorry. I have to go teach now."

She'd already put on her leather ankle boots and was stuffing her MacBook into her bag.

"Classes are canceled today due to the windstorm. I don't know much, but I know that."

She wrapped her neck in a big cotton scarf. "Still, I have things to do."

"You just can't stand it when people get emotional."

"Don't take this out on me. I never asked to be your sole lifeline to reality."

He imagined himself dressed as a minion, the suit ripped at the wrists, blood spurting.

"Wait," he said to her in a soft voice. "It still doesn't make sense."

"Things often don't."

"Everyone at the show was dismayed. Pepe Gandoya was there! Why would that be? None of them cares about Jardiner."

"They say he left a manuscript. A memoir of sorts. That's what everyone's talking about. If it were true, that would involve Mimi Whatever and many other of those degenerates who work at ¡Mañanitas! He's got all the dirt on them, on the goose with the golden eggs. Finally, an honest testimony about what goes on in the higher echelons of the network."

Benjamín was in shock. He went to the kitchen for a beer and when he came back Bárbara was gone. He smiled as he thought of the manuscript and how it terrified everyone at the network. Alicio Jardiner hadn't let him down.

The windows rattled. He smiled at the stupid wind.

Acknowledgements

Thank you to the editors of the following publications, who included stories from this book: *The Arkansas International*, *Bennington Review*, *Bodega*, *Corium Magazine*, *DIAGRAM*, *Electric Literature*'s *Recommended Reading*, *Fifth Wednesday Journal*, *Moon City Review*, *Superstition Review*, and *Washington Square Review*. Thank you to my parents for their unwavering support. Thank you to Alejandra for the Monte Elbruz office (and everything else). Thank you to the people at Indiana University's MFA program, who made me a much better writer and person than I was when they met me. Thank you to Úrsula Villarreal-Moura for generously working with me on 55.5 percent of this book. And thank you, of course, to Michael Czyzniejewski, Joel Coltharp, and Moon City Press for giving these stories a home.

MOON CITY SHORT FICTION AWARD WINNERS

2014
Cate McGowan
True Places Never Are

2015
Laura Hendrix Ezell
A Record of Our Debts

2016
Michelle Ross
There's So Much They Haven't Told You

2017
Kim Magowan
Undoing

2018
Amanda Marbais
Claiming a Body

2019
Pablo Piñero Stillmann
*Our Brains and the Brains
of Miniature Sharks*